Sara's Laughter

Also by Tom Milton

A Shower of Roses
Infamy
All the Flowers
The Admiral's Daughter
No Way to Peace

Sara's Laughter

Tom Milton

NEPPERHAN PRESS, LLC
YONKERS, NY

Published by Nepperhan Press, LLC
P.O. Box 1448, Yonkers, NY 10702
nepperhan@optonline.net
nepperhan.com

PUBLISHER'S NOTE
This is a work of fiction. Names, characters, places, and incidents
are the product of the author's imagination or are used fictitiously,
and any resemblance to actual persons, living or dead, events, or
locales is entirely coincidental.

Printed in the United States of America

Library of Congress Control Number: 2011910181

ISBN 978-0-9829904-3-8

Cover art was licensed from Publitek, Inc.

For Marie

And Sarah said: "God has brought laughter to me.
Whoever will hear of it will laugh with me."

Genesis 21:6

New York, 1993

ONE

AFTER PUTTING HER clothes on and minimally fixing her hair, Sara left the examination room and headed for the doctor's office to hear the verdict.

The door was open, and Dr. Vesely was sitting behind her desk with a faraway look in her eyes that didn't provide any clue about the situation. As usual her femininity was enhanced by her hair style and her makeup. When she saw Sara she smiled affectionately and motioned for her to come in.

Sara sat down in front of the desk with her hands folded in her lap. She felt like a student who had been summoned to the principal's office.

"Well, I'm not going to sugarcoat this," Dr. Vesely began. Except for her accent, which she may have consciously preserved, her English was perfect, and she had mastered a number of idioms, which she used profusely, maybe to offset the impersonal coldness of the medical words she had to use. "Your condition is very far advanced. Since we've tried everything else, and it hasn't worked, the only thing we have left is surgery, and there's no guarantee that it will work."

Sara had prepared herself, so she wasn't overwhelmed by the verdict, but it was still a major disappointment, and she took a while to absorb it.

Dr. Vesely waited, looking at her with compassion.

Unlike the three other doctors who had treated her, Dr. Vesely always spent time with her. She was never in a hurry to dismiss her and move on to the next patient. That was one of the many things Sara liked about her.

"What would you say my odds are if I don't have surgery?" Sara finally asked.

"I would say they're almost zero. They're not zero because there's always the possibility of a miracle."

"A miracle?" Sara laughed, not derisively but helplessly. Her eyes fixed on the gold cross that Dr. Vesely always wore around her neck. It was probably there under her scrubs when she did surgery. "You don't mean that."

"I do mean it. Things happen that science can't explain. They happen all the time. But I have to say that with your condition, the deck is stacked against a miracle."

"So I shouldn't hope for one."

"If I were you, I wouldn't."

"If you were me, would you have surgery?"

"I would," Dr. Vesely said. "I would give it a shot. I won't say you have nothing to lose because you always have risks when you have surgery. But it would be relatively noninvasive."

"What would you do?"

"I would go in through your navel with a laparoscope, and I would remove the obstruction."

"Would I have general anesthesia?"

"For this procedure it would be better than local anesthesia."

"The last time I had general anesthesia was when they took my appendix out."

"Did you have any bad effects?"

"Not that I remember. I was eighteen."

"Most of us don't remember that kind of detail from when we were eighteen. I'll write down the name of the procedure," Dr. Vesely said, reaching for a pen that had a pink costume jewel at the end of it. "Your husband will know exactly what it is."

Sara took the piece of paper, got up, and shook hands with the doctor, who observed formalities even when she had her arm halfway into your body.

While leaving the office she paused and petted the pair of Yorkshire terriers that always came to work with Dr. Vesely. One of them had a pink bow in her hair and the other had a blue one. Presumably, they were a girl and a boy.

Outside on the street she started walking toward Lexington Avenue with the intention of taking the subway down to Grand Central. Upon reaching Lexington she changed her mind and decided to walk to the station. It was thirty blocks, a mile and a half, but she needed the exercise, and she also needed time to process the latest information.

As usual there were voices in her head, not the kind of voices that Joan of Arc heard but the kind of voices that most people heard, or so she assumed.

"You shouldn't have waited so long to get married," her mother said. "Now it's too late."

"I didn't want to marry just anyone," she said. "I wanted to marry someone I loved, someone I respected, someone I could spend my life with."

"So what was wrong with Michael?"

"I didn't love him, I didn't respect him."

"And what about James?"

"He was a drip."

"Well, now you're in a fine situation," her mother told her from the grave. "And don't expect a miracle. It's not going to happen. Not to you."

And then there was her father, still alive, saying: "What did you expect from a Hispanic husband? If he were Irish, you wouldn't have a problem."

"It's not his fault. It's my fault."

"Oh, I don't believe what those doctors say. There's nothing wrong with you."

"There is," she said. "I have endometriosis."

"Take my word for it," her father said, ignoring the diagnosis. "You only have to do what normal couples do, and I'll have a grandson just like that."

"You don't want a granddaughter?"

"I already have enough women to take care of me. I want a grandson."

After a few blocks she wished she had taken the subway. The din of the cars crashing through the tunnel might have drowned out those voices.

She arrived at Grand Central in time to catch the two-twenty for Yonkers. She took a seat on the side by the river, at the window, so that she could look out and enjoy the view.

At the last minute a family of Latinos boarded the train and took the seat ahead of her, the one at the end of the car where the seats faced each other. The parents were in their late twenties, and the two children, a boy and a girl, were under five. They were all dressed up as if they had gone to church, and they probably had since it was Epiphany, or el Día de los Reyes as they called it, the day when the three kings arrived in Bethlehem to worship and bring gifts to the baby Jesus after following a star. For Latino children it was the day when they got presents, and the night before Reyes they put grass and water under their beds for the camels that the kings rode across the desert, and they left mints and cigarettes for the kings. Sara had learned about it from her husband, whose family was having a party that evening to celebrate Reyes.

Since it was a school holiday, she had made an appointment with her doctor for that day. She was conscious of the irony—on the day when people were celebrating the miraculous birth of Jesus, she had been told that it would take a miracle for her to have a baby. By a mutual understanding with her doctor, she hadn't asked what the odds would be with the surgery. Of course they would be better or the doctor wouldn't have recommended it, but how much better would they be? Would it still take a miracle for her to have a baby?

She watched the children in front of her with a mixed feeling of love and envy. They were talking in Spanish, which she understood fairly well now after being married to a Latino man for five years and teaching in schools that had a lot of Latino children. Though these two children were unable to sit still, they remained within bounds, and their behavior expressed the joy of the holiday. They were so adorable that it didn't take long for her feeling of love to obliterate her feeling of envy.

The family got off at Yonkers. She followed them out and along the platform and down the stairs. From what she had heard of their conversation, she knew they had been in the city to celebrate Reyes in the old neighborhood with grandparents, and they were coming home to Yonkers. They probably lived in the neighborhood where many of Sara's friends had grown up. At that time the neighborhood had been mainly Polish and Italian, and now it was mainly Latino.

Sara walked through the parking lot and found her car, a red Honda. She drove up Nepperhan Plaza to Warburton Avenue and then over to North Broadway, which she followed up the hill. She passed Shonnard Place, which bisected the neighborhood where her mother had grown up. Her parents had moved here almost six years ago when her mother decided they had lived in Woodlawn long enough and now they were going to live in *her* neighborhood. Though her father resisted moving to Yonkers, they finally sold the house in Woodlawn and bought a house on North Broadway. Her mother had lived there only a year, just long enough to see Sara get married.

The house on North Broadway had three bedrooms, which her mother had wanted so that both Sara and her sister Becky could spend the night there with their husbands at the same time. Neither of them had husbands yet, but when they both spent the night there for Thanksgiving, Christmas, Easter, and the Fourth of July, each of them had her own bedroom, instead of having to share a bedroom as they had at the old house, so they liked one thing about the house on North Broadway. And at least for a year their mother got to live in *her* neighborhood.

Sara parked her car in the driveway behind her father's car, a white Crown Victoria which could have been an unmarked cop car. Her father wouldn't have considered driving anything but an American car, and whenever he saw her Honda he scowled and muttered that if she had been at Guadalcanal she wouldn't have bought a Jap car.

The door was open, so after ringing the bell to warn him Sara walked in and found him in his usual location, reclining in his lounger with a bottle of Bud in one hand and a cigar in another, watching a basketball game on television. Ringer, his cat, who was regularly treated to canned tuna or fresh flounder, was asleep at his feet. Though Ringer meticulously groomed himself, he still smelled of cigar smoke, and if he was upwind of a bird or a squirrel he didn't have a chance of getting it. But as long as he got canned tuna and fresh flounder he didn't seem to mind being handicapped in his daily hunting.

As she approached him her father kept his eyes fixed on the television, and as she kissed him on the cheek he stopped her from blocking his view. His skin smelled of Ivory soap, and her skin noticed that he hadn't shaved in several days.

"How are you doing?" she asked him. She tried to remember how many days she had seen him wearing the same shirt and the same pants. He knew how to use the washing machine, but he let his dirty laundry pile up until she did it.

"I'm doing okay," he said, still not looking at her.

"What are you watching?"

"A basketball game."

"Who's playing?"

"I don't know. It's a lousy game."

"Did you drive over to Woodlawn today?"

"Yeah," he said after pausing to draw on his cigar. The word came out in a cloud of smoke. Ringer momentarily opened an eye as if to assess the chance of food.

"How was it?"

"Fine." Her father drove over to the old neighborhood Monday through Saturday, and on Sunday they went to the noon mass at St. Barnabas. They could have gone to an earlier mass but the bars didn't open until noon on Sunday, so they went later, and by the time they got out of church he could swagger into Monahan's, where he spent every day with his cronies. These were the men he had known all his life, and no one like them could be found anywhere.

"What are you having for dinner tonight?"

"Leftovers."

"You mean from Tony's?" She was referring to a Portuguese restaurant in Hastings where she and her husband took him regularly. They brought him to their house for dinner or took him to a restaurant at least once a week, and he always went home with leftovers. The night before last he had ordered the usual Roadside Chicken, which he had divided into equal halves so he would get another meal out of it. He would put the chicken in the toaster oven to warm it up. He never used the microwave she had given him. She had showed him how to use it, she had even given him a demonstration in which she warmed up a leftover piece of Roadside Chicken, but he didn't want to have anything to do with the newfangled gadget.

"I haven't heard from your sister," he said when there was a time out for a commercial. He always muted the television when they did commercials. "What's she up to?"

"I don't know. I haven't heard from her either." She assumed that Becky was busy designing, constructing, and selling new types of securities, either in New York or London, where she spent half of her time.

"I haven't seen her since Thanksgiving."

"I haven't either." She had hosted Thanksgiving for her family and her husband's family, who called it el Día de Acción de Gracias. Though Becky and her husband lived in Tribeca, in a condo they had bought several years ago for "only" three and a half million dollars, thirty minutes by car from Yonkers, they had arrived late because of traffic, and they had left early because they had to work the next day.

"Well, she should come around more often."

Sara agreed, but she didn't say so. She understood that her father was trying to make her feel responsible for her sister's failure to pay attention to him. It didn't take much since Becky was younger, four years younger, and Sara had felt responsible for Becky from the day she was born. And Becky had let her feel responsible.

Her father unmuted the television and resumed watching the basketball game.

She sat in one of the easy chairs that her mother had recovered only a month before she died. Her mother had waited years before spending the money on this project, and Sara felt bad that her mother was given so little time to enjoy the new look.

"She should have spent Christmas with us," her father said at the next commercial, giving the impression that he had been thinking about Becky the whole time.

"It wasn't our turn," Sara said.

"I don't see why they have to spend every other Christmas with his family." Her father was referring to Bart, her sister's husband, who came from Raleigh, North Carolina.

"If they spent every Christmas with us, it wouldn't be fair to Bart's family."

"It would be fair to me," her father said.

"We had a nice Christmas without them." They had taken him to have Christmas dinner with her husband's family in the Bronx. His mother had gone to the trouble to make mashed potatoes in addition to the usual rice, and it had gone well, especially after her father had discovered that her husband's father was a Yankees fan and knew a lot about baseball. At least for a while he didn't seem to mind having Christmas dinner with people who weren't white.

"Will she be around for Easter?"

"I guess so." Her sister didn't spend every other Easter with Bart's family. According to Bart's father they were Methodists. According to Bart they were Episcopalians, which had more status. Whatever they were, Easter wasn't such a big deal for Bart's family.

"Well, she better be around for Easter."

Sara laughed, remembering a conversation with her friend Regina whose mother did the same thing to her. At least twice a week Regina went to see her mother, who still lived in Woodlawn, and her mother spent most of the time complaining that her other children didn't come to see her. Regina finally told her mother: "*I came to see you. So what am I, chopped liver?*"

"That sounds like a Jewish expression," her mother said. "Where did you learn it?"

Though it wasn't true, Regina almost said: "From the Jewish guy I'm having an affair with."

During the next commercial her father asked: "How was school today?"

"We didn't have school today. It's a holiday."

"Oh, that's right. It's Epiphany. They give you the day off for that?"

"It's a major holiday for Latinos. Half the students wouldn't have shown up, so they decided not to have school."

"You mean half your students are—" He stopped short of using the word that he must have realized would offend her. "What do you call them?"

"Latinos," she told him.

"What are they doing here?"

"They're trying to make a better life for themselves and for their children."

Her father took a swig of beer. "They don't belong here."

"That's what they said about the Irish."

"They never said that about us. If we hadn't come here, who would have done the work?"

"If the Latinos hadn't come here, who would be doing the work now?"

"The people they're taking jobs away from."

"And who are they?"

"I don't know. But they must be taking jobs away from people." He unmuted the television and resumed watching the basketball game.

"Well, I came to see if you're all right," Sara said, deciding it was almost time to leave.

"I'm all right. But I need some things."

"Why didn't you tell me? I could have stopped and bought them on the way."

"I didn't know I needed them."

It was the usual game. If he had called her and told her what he needed, then he wouldn't have her on the hook for a return visit. Of course she saw him every day anyway. She had moved from the city and bought a house within walking distance so that she could see him every day. But he evidently didn't want to give her the option of skipping a day.

She found the list on the kitchen table along with a pile of mail. For some reason he had fallen prey to the firms that sell elderly people things they don't need and would never dream of buying if they weren't offered the deal of a lifetime. He had subscriptions to a lot of women's magazines, including *Glamour, Mademoiselle, Good Housekeeping,* and *Ladies' Home Journal.* He didn't even read men's magazines, except for *Playboy,* and that he didn't actually read, he just examined the pictures of the Playmate of the Month. He gave the women's magazines to his daughters as if they were rewards for good behavior.

The list of things he needed wasn't that long, and there wasn't anything on it that he couldn't have bought himself on Palisade Avenue, a block away. But he expected her to run errands for him, just as he expected women to do everything for him. If he hadn't been the only boy, the last child of parents who had four girls ahead of him, her father wouldn't have been so spoiled. But what could she do about it? She couldn't change him, and whenever she resisted his demands he made her feel like a bad daughter.

"You're enabling him," a voice in her head told her.

"No, I'm not," she retorted. "He was enabled long before I arrived on the scene."

She picked up the list and put it into her handbag. She looked around the kitchen and saw dirty dishes in the sink, waiting for her to do them. She was influenced by that voice enough to leave them there, at least for now.

"So when am I going to have a grandson?" her father asked when she returned to the living room. The television was muted for another commercial.

"When God decides to give you one," Sara replied.

"Oh, don't give me that. You're not married to God, you're married to a—" Again he stopped short of saying it. "What's the matter with him?"

"There's nothing the matter with him."

"I thought colored people were well hung. Is that a myth?"

Sara controlled herself, but her anger was rising. "Dad, I'm leaving. I'm not going to listen to you making racial slurs about my husband."

"I wasn't making a racial slur about your husband," her father said, backing off a little.

"What were you doing?"

"I was just expressing my frustration."

"Well, you should find another way to express it."

"Personally, I like the guy. I think he would have made a great baseball player. Dominicans have fast hands, so they play well in the infield."

"Where do the Irish play well?"

"We play well everywhere."

"Then why haven't there been more Irish baseball stars?"

"There've been hundreds of Irish baseball stars. What do you think Babe Ruth was?"

"I don't know. Was he Irish?"

"Of course he was. All the big stars were Irish," her father asserted forcefully, "until they started letting colored people into the game."

"I didn't know that Joe DiMaggio was Irish." Remembering how in the old neighborhood an Italian boy had confided to her that when he grew up he wanted to be a white man, she realized that she had given her father an opening.

But her father didn't take it. He only said: "There were some good Italians, but all the big stars in those days were Irish."

Her husband would have pointed out that the big stars now were Latinos, but she didn't know enough about baseball to make the case. At least she had distracted her father from putting the blame on her husband for their inability to have a child.

"I have to go," Sara said, hoping for once to get off lightly.

"Where are you going?" her father asked. He always tried to stop her from leaving with the implication that she had nothing better to do than to take care of him.

"I'm going home. And then I'm going to a party."

"Where?" Her father acted as if she were a teenager needing his permission.

"In the Bronx. Marcelo's family is celebrating Reyes."

"You mean Epiphany. If you don't watch out, you'll end up speaking their language."

"I already do. *Te amo, papá, pero a veces puedes ser muy difícil.*"

"I understood that. You don't think I did, but I did."

"Well, in case you didn't, I said I love you, Papa, but at times you can be very difficult."

"I know," he admitted. He gazed at the muted television sadly. "I miss your mother. At times she was a pain in the ass, but I loved her. I still love her. And I'm still mad at God for taking her away from me."

"I'm sorry," she murmured, softening.

"If I bug you about giving me a grandson, it's only because it would make me so happy."

"I understand. I'm doing everything I can." She hesitated, and then she said: "I'm probably going to have surgery."

"Surgery?" He looked alarmed. "What for?"

"To correct the problem."

"What problem?"

"I keep telling you," Sara said patiently, "it's not Marcelo's fault we can't have a baby. They tested him, and he's fine. It's my fault. I have endometriosis."

"What the hell is that?"

She decided not to go into the details since her father was squeamish about feminine matters. Once, while looking for a contact lens she had dropped in the bathroom, he had spotted it on top of a carton of tampons, and he let her retrieve it, afraid to touch the carton. "It's an obstruction inside me that stops me from getting pregnant."

"How did it get there?" her father asked as if he were ready to kill whoever was responsible for it being there.

"It grew there."

"Why?"

"They don't know why."

"Well, why did it happen to *you*?"

"I ask that question over and over." She had not only asked the doctors, but she had also asked God. "And all they can say is, it happens to a lot of women."

"Is it like cancer?"

"No. It won't kill me. But as long as it's there, I can't get pregnant."

Her father puffed on the cigar, thinking. "How do you know your doctor's right?"

"I don't know. But I have faith in her."

"Your doctor's a woman?"

"She's one of the best. She treats the wives of a lot of famous people."

"That doesn't mean she knows what she's doing. I think you should get a second opinion."

"I already did. In fact, she's my fourth opinion."

Her father flicked the ash off his cigar, missing the ashtray. Ringer raised his head, twitching his ears as if some ash had landed on him. "You know what I think? I think those doctors are taking you for a ride. It's all about money. They don't give a shit about you."

"The doctor I have now cares about me."

"Aw, I don't believe it. And how could a woman possibly be a good doctor?"

So much for getting off lightly. "Dad, you're entitled to your opinions. If you think women aren't good for anything but waiting on you, then I'm not going to argue with you. But at some point I may stop waiting on you."

"You wouldn't do that to your father."

"Don't push me. I have my own problems to worry about."

Her father took a swig of beer and shifted his foot, which disturbed the cat.

Ringer finally sat up and yawned and then looked at her father expectantly. No doubt the cat had canned tuna or fresh flounder on his mind.

"I still think," her father said, ignoring the cat but not facing her, "that if you and your husband do what normal couples do, you'll have a baby."

"Just like that."

"Yeah. Just like that."

"All right. Then you can help me."

"How?" he asked, looking puzzled but interested.

"You can pray every day to the Blessed Mother and ask her for a miracle."

"Oh, you don't need a miracle to have a baby."

"Most women don't. But I do. So will you pray for me?"

"Sure," he finally said. "She owes me one."

She backed out of her father's driveway and got onto North Broadway. She passed St. Brigid, the church and the school where she taught third grade. She turned left on Morsemere and headed down the hill toward the river, into the network of switch-backing streets that formed the neighborhood of Woodstock, though that name wasn't used much by the people who lived there. When they moved to Yonkers she and Marcelo picked the location carefully. It was near enough to her father so that they could take care of him but not near enough so that he could interfere with them. The house they had bought with the proceeds of selling their condo in the city was a Victorian, eighty years old but in good condition and just the perfect size for them. It had three bedrooms, one for them and two for the children they hoped to have, or enough bedrooms for four children if they had two of each gender. And there were two full bathrooms, though they needed some work.

The house was on the side of the hill, where the street doubled back to continue the descent to Warburton, the street that ran along the river. From their living room, their dining room, and their bedroom they had unobstructed views of the river. They were five minutes from St. Brigid, and less than ten minutes from her father. And Marcelo was only twenty minutes from the clinic where he worked in the Bronx.

She was glad to see Marcelo's car parked in the driveway. She knew he had come home early so that he would be there for her when she returned from the doctor, and she was grateful. She thanked God for sending her Marcelo. When her friends, who had wondered what kind of man she would finally marry, met Marcelo they were unanimous in their judgment: she had done well to wait for the right man.

In the kitchen she found Marcelo at the table having a cup of coffee, the Santo Domingo brand they could find only at stores in the Bronx.

He immediately got up, and seeing her face, which wasn't good at hiding things, he opened his arms and enfolded her in them, holding her close.

With her face pressed against his shoulder she let the tears flow freely.

He didn't have to ask her about the verdict.

"I'm sorry," she told him, "I'm so sorry. I love you so much, and I want so much to have your children."

"It's all right," he assured her. "I didn't marry you just to have children. I married you to have you."

"I know," she said, kissing his neck. "And I married you for the same reason."

"So what exactly did the doctor say?"

"She said that the only thing left is surgery."

"What kind of surgery?"

Sara got the piece of paper out of her handbag and handed it to her husband.

Marcelo read what the doctor had written. "A laparoscopy? That makes sense. Did she explain it to you?"

"Yes. And she said that without the surgery, the odds of my

having a baby are almost zero. They're not zero because there's always the possibility of a miracle."

"Then we'll pray for a miracle," he said, folding the piece of paper. "But if it doesn't happen, we'll still have each other."

"We will," she said, giving thanks.

They sealed the thanks with a long kiss. It led them into the bedroom where they did what her father recommended.

Maybe it was all that talk about miracles, or maybe it was something she had eaten at the party, but that night Sara had a dream in which she heard the voice of God telling her husband: "Your wife Sara will have a baby."

She awoke and laughed.

TWO WEEKS BEFORE Christmas she had run into her friend Regina while getting off the train at the Yonkers station. Together, they grew up in Woodlawn, went to St. Barnabas, and then went to Fordham. They stayed in touch during the time when they both worked in the city but lost track of each other after they got married. In fact, when they accidently met at the train station they hadn't seen each other since Regina's wedding almost four years ago.

Now they were both living in Yonkers, though in different neighborhoods. Regina lived near the racetrack in a predominantly Italian neighborhood, where she and her husband Joe shared a two-family house with his parents. Regina, after a career in the media, was now a counselor at St. Barnabas, and Joe owned a business that remodeled houses.

They had found time before they were swallowed up by the holidays to have lunch together and do some catching up. They had gone to a restaurant on Nepperhan Avenue that they figured was equally distant from their homes. It was called Angelo's, and it had been recommended by one of Joe's relatives from Bari, which meant a lot since people from Italy rarely had anything good to say about the food that Americans considered Italian. Though not from Italy, the owner and chef was from Argentina, which apparently was the next best thing.

Since they had been raised on meat and potatoes, Sara and Regina didn't pretend to know about food. While working in the city they had been exposed to different cuisines, but they had mostly gone to Italian restaurants. So they were comfortable with Italian food, and they were reassured by the fact that someone who knew food liked Angelo's.

Sara and Regina met there for lunch on the Saturday after Epiphany. Regina got there first and was seated at a corner table dreamily inhaling her cigarette when Sara arrived. Regina had been smoking since she was thirteen. She didn't believe the government warnings about the harmful effects of this habit. She believed these warnings were intended to get people to shift their addiction from tobacco to cocaine, in which the government had a major interest.

The two friends were very different in appearance. When they were in high school they both wished they looked like the other: Sara wished she had blond hair and blue eyes, while Regina wished she had dark hair and dark eyes. But neither of them had ever tried to fulfill her wish by dyeing her hair or wearing lenses that changed her eye color.

In addition to their common background of growing up in Woodlawn and going to the same Catholic schools, they discovered at their lunch before Christmas that they had several present things in common. They had both dropped out of corporate life, they were both now involved in education, they were both taking care of an aging parent, and they were both having trouble getting pregnant.

After carefully setting her cigarette in an ashtray Regina got up and came around the table to greet Sara, and they gave each other a long, close hug.

"How are you doing?" Regina asked with tender concern. She had a way of looking at you very directly, without filters.

"I'm fine," Sara said. "How are you?"

"Well, I'm trying to rebuild my self-esteem after having it destroyed last night by Joe's mother. But other than that, I'm in good shape."

They sat down, which signaled the waiter to come over and ask them if they wanted a drink. Regina ordered a vodka martini, while Sara had a white wine.

"What did his mother do to you?" Sara asked when the waiter had left them.

Regina sighed and picked up her cigarette. She took a long drag, exhaled the smoke, and then said: "She did what she always does. She made me feel I'm not good enough for her son."

"How did she do that?"

"The sauce."

"The sauce? What do you mean?"

"Well, I should have said the gravy. That's what they call it. But it's not gravy like you and I would put on meat or chicken or turkey. It's pasta sauce."

"What's the problem?"

"The problem is, I don't know how to make it."

"Has she told you how to make it?"

"Many times. And I swear, I make it the same way she does. I use the same ingredients, and I cook them the same, but Joe says it doesn't taste the same as his mother's sauce."

"Does she agree with him?"

"Oh, yeah. She comes upstairs and tastes the sauce and spits it out, saying how could I feed this poison to her son?"

Sara laughed. "And what does he do?"

"He enjoys it. He likes having women fight over him."

"He sounds like my father."

"Or my father, God rest his soul. I thought Irish men were the worst, but now I'm beginning to wonder. Is your husband spoiled like that?"

"No, not really."

"You're very lucky," Regina said, flicking the ash off her cigarette. "Don't get me wrong. I love my husband, but I wish he'd separate himself from his mother."

It sounded as if Regina was applying a concept she had learned from the psychology she had studied in order to get her master's in counseling. "Well, maybe it would help if you didn't share a house with his parents."

"It definitely would. I keep suggesting that we buy our own house, but Joe keeps saying he wants to wait until his business is established."

"How long will that take?"

"As long as he wants."

At that point the waiter brought their drinks and asked if they were ready to order.

Sara planned to cook *arroz con pollo* for dinner that evening, so she avoided the chicken dishes. She decided on a veal dish since it was something she wouldn't cook at home.

Regina ordered the *bistecca*.

The room was filling with men in suits who probably worked at City Hall or for the firms that served the government. There were only a few large private employers left in Yonkers after the departure of J.P. Stephens and Otis Elevator.

Regina took a sip of her martini. "Ah, this reminds me of working in the city. Going to lunch and making deals. Sometimes I miss it."

"I don't," Sara said. "I mean, I miss being in my twenties, but not the work."

"We had some wild times," Regina said with a wicked smile. "Remember how we used to worry about getting pregnant?"

"If only we'd known, we wouldn't have committed a sin by taking birth control pills."

"You mean an additional sin. We weren't married to those guys we slept with."

Regina talked as if there had been a lot of guys, but there really hadn't been. Sara had slept with only three guys, and she had intended to marry the first one—until she found out that he was sleeping with another girl at the same time. After hearing what he had done to her Regina cursed him, and then took Sara out and got drunk with her, sharing her pain.

"But I believe," Regina said, "that God forgave us. I mean, He must have understood how sheltered we were."

"Are the girls at St. Barnabas still sheltered?"

"I guess they still are, but compared with us they're very experienced."

"When I look at my students, my heart goes out to them. They have no idea what's going to happen to them."

"I still have no idea what's going to happen to me."

"What does your doctor say?" Sara asked, knowing what Regina meant.

"He says I should keep trying to have a baby. He says there's nothing wrong with me. But Joe's mother," Regina continued, "believes there's something wrong with me. I mean, besides the fact that I can't make sauce."

"You're the psychologist. Isn't that what the sauce is about?"

"Of course it is. If I had a baby boy, my sauce would be perfect. If I had a girl, it would be acceptable."

"So she'd accept a girl?"

"Yeah. She'd see it as evidence that I could have a baby, and that a boy might follow."

"My father wanted to have a son, but he never did. So he wants to make up for it by having a grandson."

Regina took another sip of her martini. "I wonder why our fathers never realized that the best thing that happened to them was having daughters."

"Maybe they realized it but wouldn't admit it."

"Maybe. But I think men are just too dumb to know what's good for them."

"Except our husbands."

"Except them," Regina agreed. "Whatever I say about men, it doesn't apply to our husbands."

"But it does apply to our fathers."

"It does. Well, at least we were both smart enough not to marry men like our fathers."

"Or lucky enough."

"No. We were smart. We didn't marry the first guy who came along, or the guy our mothers wanted us to marry. We waited for the right guy."

"If I'd married the guy my mother wanted me to marry, I'd be divorced now."

"Like so many of our friends. Did you hear that Mary Logan and her husband split?"

"I didn't hear that. They have three children, don't they?"

"Yeah. I guess that proves that having children doesn't save a marriage."

"We were taught that having children was the purpose of marriage. So if having them doesn't save a marriage, then maybe not having them won't wreck a marriage."

"It won't wreck our marriages. I might have to kill Joe's mother, and you might have to kill your father, but we're not going to let them drive us apart from our husbands."

"You should hear what my father calls my husband. Or almost calls him. He always stops short of the word, but I know what it is."

"If my father had lived," Regina said, "I know what he would have called Joe."

"My third grade students aren't like that. We have white and black and brown kids, and they don't seem to notice the differences."

"My high school students aren't like that either."

"So something positive has happened."

The waiter brought their food, and they started eating.

"Going back to the subject," Regina said, cutting her steak. "What's happening with you?"

"My doctor recommended surgery," Sara said.

"Are you going to have it?"

"It's the only thing left."

"There's adoption."

"I know. But I only want to do that as a last resort. And I have this feeling that if we do adopt a baby, we'll be taking her away from her mother."

"I notice you made the baby a female."

"Females are what's available for adoption," Sara said, "because those dumb men we were talking about don't want them. They only want males."

Regina chewed. "Well, taking a baby away from her mother might be good for the baby."

"It might be. But it would be bad for the mother."

"It wouldn't be so bad if the mother didn't want the baby."

"No matter how much she didn't want it, I think when she saw it she'd change her mind."

"But you haven't ruled out adoption."

"I haven't ruled out anything."

"I have to admit," Regina said after swallowing and taking a sip of water, "that Joe would have trouble adopting a baby. He wants his own blood."

"I understand. I want my own blood."

"What about Marcelo?"

"He's not hung up on that. He believes I'd make a good mother, and he believes I'd be happy having children. That's why he wants them."

"God bless Marcelo. If I could get Joe away from his mother, he'd be the same way."

"Then you have a goal, a proximate goal."

Regina smiled. "At least we learned the vocabulary of the corporate world. Do you think we learned anything else?"

"I think we learned to pursue goals."

"I guess we did. They weren't worth pursuing, but we learned how to do it. That's what got us through graduate school."

They ate in a comfortable silence for a while.

Then Sara said: "You remember how I used to hear voices?"

"Oh, yeah. Like Joan of Arc."

"I still hear them. I mean, they're usually the voices of my mother or my father telling me I did something wrong, or warning me about something."

"I'm glad I don't hear voices like those."

"But last night I had a dream, and I heard the voice of God telling my husband I would have a baby."

"Did God say if it would be a son or daughter?"

"No. He just said a baby."

"How do you know it was the voice of God?"

"It wasn't my father, so who else could it have been?"

"It could have been Satan tempting you."

"Yeah. But I don't think it was."

"Well, I hope your dream comes true," Regina said, reaching out across the table for Sara's hands. "I hope and I pray that it comes true."

"Thank you," Sara said, clasping hands with her friend.

Her father had been born and raised in Woodlawn, a unique neighborhood in the Bronx. His mother and father and the five children lived in the top half of a two-family house, and his father's parents, who had immigrated from Ireland, lived in the bottom half. It was said that if you were an immigrant from Ireland you would feel more at home in Woodlawn than in any other neighborhood of New York City.

In his senior year of high school her father dropped out and joined the marines. It was right after the attack on Pearl Harbor, and he spent the next four years fighting in the Pacific. He was involved in several island assaults, but he was proudest of fighting in the battle of Guadalcanal with the marines who stopped a superior force of Japanese from retaking a crucial airfield. In his mind that battle was the turning point in the war, and after that the Japanese were no longer on the attack but in retreat. In the fighting he received a serious wound in his right leg for which he was awarded the Purple Heart, and he claimed that there was still a piece of shrapnel in his leg that enabled him to anticipate changes in weather.

When he returned from the war he got a job as a lineman at the phone company, which despite the injury to his leg he was able to perform until a few years before he retired. His father had also worked for the phone company, which welcomed Irish immigrants and their progeny. For almost ten years he was a happy bachelor until the secretary he was dating finally gave him an ultimatum. She worked at the head office, and he had met her while trying to resolve a problem with his benefits. So they got married and moved into the top half of the two-family house, with his parents in the bottom half.

Within a year they had Sara, and four years later, after losing a baby, they had Rebecca. They wanted more children, but for some reason her mother stopped getting pregnant, and that was it. They never had the son her father wanted.

As she was growing up in Woodlawn, Sara saw her father as the king of the heap. Not only did everyone in the neighborhood know him, but also everyone deferred to him. It was as if he had something that everyone wanted, and everyone bestowed favors on him, including endless rounds of free drinks, in the hope of receiving whatever it was.

Of course her father was a Yankees fan. In that era most of the games were played in the day, but her father and his buddies at the phone company were somehow always able to get off work for the game. They were somehow always able to get tickets, not in the bleachers but in choice locations. Years later Sara realized that her father must have had connections, but at the time she believed along with most people that it was simply the luck of the Irish.

Not wanting to be an only child, Sara welcomed her baby sister, and though she was just four at the time she immediately assumed responsibility for Becky. She helped her mother take care of Becky as much as she could, and she imagined having a close relationship with her sister. But as they grew older their differences got in the way.

Sara was pretty, and unlike most girls she never doubted that she was pretty. It helped that boys were always reinforcing this belief by paying attention to her, but it was innate, so it didn't depend on their attention. Sara had been born with self-esteem, a solid confidence in herself that nothing had shaken, whereas her sister had been born without it. There was no way of explaining this difference, and there was apparently no way of eliminating it.

As much as Sara tried to instill a feeling of self-esteem in her sister by encouraging her and praising her, Becky resisted her, and to compensate for her negative feelings about herself she was aggressive and even malicious. When she was five she began to disfigure Sara's dolls, smashing their faces and pulling out their hair and tearing their clothes and breaking their limbs, and she continued being destructive to Sara's possessions. When she was fifteen she scrawled graffiti over the photographs of Sara's friends in her high school yearbook.

Sara never told her parents about these things, and she didn't complain to Becky about them since the damage was done. But she did complain after Becky interfered in her relationship with a boy. The boy went to Fordham Prep, and he had invited Sara to a dance. Sara wasn't in love with the boy, but she liked him, and she was looking forward to the event.

The day before the dance the boy called her and told her he was sick, so he couldn't go. She told him she was sorry, she hoped he would feel better. She spent the night of the dance watching television with her family.

The next day Regina called her and asked her why she wasn't at the dance.

"My date got sick," Sara explained, "so he couldn't go."

"I thought you were going with Jerry O'Donnell."

"I was, but he got sick."

"Really? He didn't look sick when I saw him at the dance, but he did look drunk."

"You saw him at the dance?"

"Yeah. He was there."

"Was he with anyone?"

"No, he was alone. And he didn't look happy. I heard he really likes you."

Sara was puzzled. "Then why would he have called me and told me he was sick?"

"I can't imagine. But I'll find out."

She probably should have stopped Regina, but she wanted to get to the bottom of it.

They were in the hallway at school when Regina explained what had happened. "Your dear sister told his sister that the only reason you accepted his invitation to the dance was so you could see another guy there."

"What other guy? There's no other guy."

"Well, he must have believed it. And it must have hurt his feelings."

Sara felt really bad for Jerry, who was a nice boy, so the first thing she did was call him and tell him that there had been a misunderstanding.

"Whatever you heard," she told him, "it wasn't true. And I'm sorry we didn't go to the dance together. We would have had a good time."

"I'm sorry I believed my sister," he said. "I should have known a girl like you would never do a thing like that."

"If you want to go to the movies sometime, just call me."

"I will. Thanks." And he did call her. They dated for a while and became good friends.

Meanwhile, she had to confront her sister. She waited until they were alone in the kitchen a few days later having a snack before going to bed.

"I heard you made up a story about me," Sara began.

"I don't know what you're talking about," Becky told her, chewing a cookie.

"The story for Jerry O'Donnell."

Becky's face twitched. "I still don't know what you're talking about."

"The story that the only reason I accepted his invitation to the dance was so I could see another guy there."

"I didn't make up a story like that."

"His sister says you did."

"She's lying."

"Why would she lie?"

"Because she doesn't like me."

Sara now felt bad for her sister, and she tried to help her by saying: "Did it ever occur to you that if you were nicer to people they'd be nicer to you?"

"I'm nice to them. They just don't like me."

"Well, how do you think your story made Jerry feel?"

"I don't know. And I don't care."

"Then his sister isn't lying."

"Maybe she isn't. What difference does it make?"

"It makes a lot of difference to me. I'm your sister, and you did something to interfere with my relationship with Jerry."

"You don't love him."

"Maybe I don't, but I like him," Sara said, "and I would have had a good time with him."

"Then you were using him."

"I wasn't using him. It's not a big deal going to a dance with someone."

"If it's not, then why are you bugging me about it?"

"Because it hurt me."

"Then you know what it's like."

"Did I do something that hurt you?"

"You don't have to," Becky said, beginning to cry. "It hurts just being your sister."

"I'm sorry," Sara said, going to her sister and putting her arms around her. "I'm sorry it hurts, and I wish I could do something about it."

"You can't. So don't try."

On her way home from the restaurant Sara decided to go to the Korean grocer in Dobbs Ferry, where she could get fresh fruit and vegetables, so she drove east on Yonkers Avenue and got onto the Saw Mill River Parkway going north. She got off at the Ashford Avenue exit and headed west toward Dobbs Ferry. After passing the community hospital she saw a group of protesters standing out in front of the clinic where they did abortions. From early in the morning until late at night they were always there with signs that said things like "Stop the murder!" and "Respect the rights of the unborn" and "Life begins at the moment of conception."

Sara agreed with their position, believing it was morally wrong for a woman to end a life that she had conceived through the grace of God. She also had a personal feeling that she wasn't proud of—her resentment of the fact that the women seeking abortions here had been able to get pregnant so easily. They had no idea how lucky they were. She tried to offset this ugly feeling by mustering empathy for them, especially for the young girls who didn't know what they were doing, and she always said a prayer for them, asking God to forgive them.

She stopped at the grocer, made her purchases, and then continued home.

Marcelo had returned from his Saturday morning hours at the clinic, and he was relaxing in the living room with the radio tuned to a Latino station. They were playing a *merengue*, and roused by the energetic beat she set her bags of produce on the kitchen counter and moved across the floor toward her husband, who got up and took her into his arms.

They had learned to maneuver around the furniture, though you didn't have to wander very far while doing a *merengue*. As one of their Dominican friends had told her, you simply did in a vertical position what you felt like doing horizontally.

As usual the music kept going until you thought it would never end, but they kept dancing since they prided themselves on never stopping before the music did.

When it finally ended they collapsed on the sofa and lay back.

"That was a good one," Sara said, catching her breath.

"It was," he agreed. "It makes me want to go to the island."

"Me too." They tried to go there once a year to see his aunts and uncles and cousins, and maybe they would get there after school was out for the summer. She loved being there with his extended family, and she always looked forward to it.

"How was Regina?"

"She was fine. I'm so glad we met at the station."

"It's good to pick up with old friends."

"It's like you saw them only last week. You don't have to build a relationship."

"It's like that with the guys I grew up with." He got together with them once a month, usually on Saturdays after his hours at the clinic. They went to a Dominican restaurant in the Bronx where they feasted on *chivo* or *carne mechada* or *sancocho*, washed down with Presidente beer, right from the bottle, and digested with Brugal rum, straight up.

"Regina also waited for the right guy," Sara said, "and now she's also having trouble getting pregnant."

"Does she know why she can't get pregnant?"

"No. Her doctor says there's nothing wrong with her."

"Her doctor couldn't know that for sure." He could make this statement with authority as a graduate of Cornell Medical School, a physician at New York Hospital, and now a family practitioner who served the people from his old neighborhood by working at a clinic there. He didn't make a lot of money, but he wasn't doing it for money, he was doing it to help people.

"Her doctor could be right. I mean, her problem could be psychological. They live with his parents, and his mother puts a lot of pressure on her."

"Your father puts a lot of pressure on you."

"I can handle that. It's not my problem."

There was a silence while they confronted her problem, and then he asked: "Have you made a decision about the surgery?"

"I have. But tell me," Sara said. "If you were my doctor and not my husband, would you recommend the surgery?"

"If I were your doctor, I'd recommend it. Not because I think it'll solve the problem, but because if you don't try it you'll feel you didn't do everything you possibly could."

"That's why I decided to try it."

"I understand. And then you will have tried everything."

"You mean everything the church allows."

"If you want to try other things, I'll go along with them. But I don't want you to do them for me."

"Well, let's take one thing at a time."

"Okay. You should ask Dr. Vesely to schedule you first in the line of procedures she does that day. You want her to be fresh. Of course if one of her patients goes into labor that morning, the birth will have priority."

"If that happens, I'll gladly give up my place in line."

"I know you will. That's why I love you," Marcelo said. "You always think about other people."

"Not always. But I'm happier when I do."

Marcelo put his arm around her and drew her close, saying: "I hope the surgery solves the problem. But if it doesn't, we can always adopt children."

She was grateful to him for saying this. It relieved some of the pressure on her. But it also made her want even more to have his children.

THREE

THE NEXT DAY they drove her father to the noon mass at St. Barnabas. Sara had once suggested that they go to St. Brigid, which was only a few blocks from where they lived, instead of driving across the county. But her father absolutely refused to consider it, and she imagined that her mother had only once suggested that they go to St. Brigid. Though her father had moved against his will to Yonkers, there were two places in Woodlawn that he wouldn't let go of—one was Monahan's, and the other was St. Barnabas.

Marcelo as always was very accommodating with her father. Since her father wouldn't ride in a Japanese car, Marcelo left his car in front of her father's house and drove the Crown Victoria, with her father sitting in the passenger seat and giving him directions not only how to get to the church, which they had done hundreds of times, but also how to drive the car and even how to live his life. Marcelo was always respectful, coming from a culture that automatically respected older people, but he didn't let her father push him around. There were lines that he wouldn't let her father cross, and her father, having tested him, respected these lines. Of course it helped that Marcelo was a male and a Yankees fan.

They always sat in what her father considered his own pew, the seventh row from the front, with Marcelo inside, Sara in the middle, and her father on the aisle. He knew almost everyone in the church, and during the collection the ushers would pause ever so slightly to pay their respects as they swung the basket in front of him. There were also some people that Sara had gone to school with, though most of them had left the neighborhood.

Regina wasn't there since she now attended church with her husband's family at St. Ann.

During the mass her father was a different person—humble, tractable, and considerate. It showed that he had these qualities, and Sara wished he would display them more often. When they exchanged the sign of peace he hugged her very tenderly while reaching his hand over her shoulder to take Marcelo's extended hand.

As she knelt after receiving communion she prayed as usual with her forehead against her clasped hands, which hid her face and gave her privacy and prevented her from being distracted by the people going back to their seats. She had a list of people that she regularly prayed for, starting with the soul of her mother and ending with herself. In the middle she prayed for Becky and she asked God for a better relationship with her sister. Of course she prayed for Marcelo, even though he didn't need her prayers. And she prayed that the dream in which she had heard the voice of God telling her husband she would have a baby would come true. Unnecessarily, she made sure that God understood she would be as happy with a son or a daughter.

After church they had brunch as usual at Monahan's. As St. Barnabas was the neighborhood's soul, this Irish bar was the neighborhood's heart, and among Sara's earliest memories were being at Monahan's with her father. She could remember him standing her on top of the bar—she must have been three—and saying with pride: "Did you ever see a prettier girl?"

Sara and Marcelo went ahead and occupied a booth while her father stopped to greet people along the way. Though he had seen these people only yesterday, he acted as if he hadn't seen them in twenty years, and he took his time getting to the booth.

By then Sara had ordered for him. She knew what he wanted since he always had the same thing—two eggs scrambled, bacon, home fries, and whole wheat toast. And he always had the two drinks that came with the brunch.

When he sat down Sara could feel the bench of the wooden booth rising beneath her from the leverage of his weight. Her father had no fat on him, but he was a big, heavy man.

"What the hell is this supposed to be?" he asked after tasting his Bloody Mary.

"It's a Bloody Mary," Sara told him.

"It's not a Bloody Mary. It has no vodka in it." He turned and raised his arm and yelled like a drill sergeant: "Denny, come here!"

A handsome young waiter rushed to his service. "Yes, Mr. Quinlan. Is there a problem?"

"This drink you call a Bloody Mary has no vodka in it."

"I'm sorry. I'll fix it." The waiter, who had an Irish accent, reached for the glass.

Her father held him by the wrist. "You don't believe me?"

"I do believe you," the waiter said, immobilized. "I'll ask the bartender to put some vodka in it."

"Tell him I didn't order the kind of Bloody Mary with no vodka in it. What do you call it?"

"A Virgin Mary," the waiter said.

"That's sacrilegious. You shouldn't call it that. You should call it Spiced Tomato Juice."

"I'll suggest that," the waiter said, waiting for her father to release his hand, which he finally did. The waiter took the offending drink away.

"These immigrants have a lot to learn," her father said.

"So did your grandparents."

"It's different now. My grandparents came and stayed here. These kids go back and forth."

"They probably miss their families."

"Well, they should either come here or stay there."

Instead of citing the example of his own family, Marcelo wisely steered the conversation to a safe topic. "What do you think about the trade for Abbott?"

The Yankees had traded a first-base prospect, a right-handed starter, and a left-handed reliever with the Angels for Jim Abbott, a young left-handed starter.

"They gave away too much for him."

"But they need to strengthen the rotation."

"Rotation," her father sneered. "In the old days the pitchers didn't rotate. They played as often as necessary."

"They must have taken days off."

"Yeah, one day off. And they pitched nine innings. They didn't send in a reliever unless the pitcher was injured. And they didn't call him a 'starting' pitcher. They expected him to pitch the whole game."

"I guess pitchers were in better shape back then."

"They sure as hell were. These kids playing ball today are—" Out of deference to Sara he stopped short of saying the word. He finally said: "They're not real men."

"So you think they didn't make a good trade to get Abbott."

"Well, I'll say this much for him—the guy has balls. Did you know he was born without a right hand?"

"I didn't know that," Marcelo said, though he probably did. He was giving her father the opportunity to know something that most people didn't know.

"So he had balls to pursue a career in baseball and make it to the big leagues."

"Would you say he's a real man?"

"Yeah. I'd say he is. But I still think we gave away too much for him."

The waiter returned with a Bloody Mary that presumably had been fortified with vodka. Before commenting, her father tasted it. "That's better."

A few minutes later their food arrived.

"Have you heard from Becky?" her father asked after eating a forkful of eggs.

"No. Have you?"

"I never hear from her."

Sara only heard from her when Becky wanted something, but she didn't say it since her prayer for a better relationship with her sister was fresh in her mind. Nor did she suggest that her father call her sister. Though he had worked all his life for the phone company, he didn't have much use for telephones.

"Maybe we should have them to dinner," Marcelo suggested. "I'll make paella."

"I like your payella," her father said.

"I'll call her and see if they're free next weekend," Sara said. Though they didn't have much of a social life, Becky and Bart always seemed to have commitments when Sara invited them to dinner. To be fair, Becky traveled a lot, and she used weekends to recover. But she could have spared a few hours now and then on a Saturday evening to see her father.

"How long have they been married?" her father asked.

"A little over three years." Until their mother died, her sister hadn't shown much interest in acquiring a husband, but then she found a man and married him within a year. She had met him in a bar, and she had been impressed by the presents he gave her. Sara was sure that her mother wouldn't have approved of Bart. Had Becky married him in a panic after losing her mother? Or had she then felt free to marry a man of her own choosing?

"Well, she should have had a baby by now."

"They're probably not trying yet."

"You don't have to try," her father said as if he were giving a lesson in sex education. "You only have to do what normal couples do, and you have a baby."

"Just like that," Sara murmured.

"They might be trying not to have a baby," Marcelo said.

"You mean by using the rhythm method?"

"Yeah. Or by using contraceptives."

Looking alarmed, her father confronted Sara and asked: "Is your sister using contraceptives?"

"I have no idea what she's doing."

"Well, you should talk with her about that."

"Do you really think she'd listen to me?"

"You're her older sister."

"Yeah. I know. Did you listen to your older sisters?"

"They were girls," her father said. "They didn't have anything useful to tell me."

"If that's how you felt about your older sisters," Sara said, "then you should be able to imagine how Becky feels about *her* older sister."

Her father looked as if he didn't understand. He dropped the subject to eat some home fries, and then he picked it up again. "Does she go to church?"

"I don't know." She did know, but she didn't want to upset her father. Bart wasn't a Catholic and Becky wasn't an Episcopalian, or whatever Bart pretended to be, so they couldn't go to church together, and they didn't want to go separately.

"If she doesn't," her father said, "it's not good."

"Well, why don't you talk with her about it?"

"How can I talk with her? I never see her."

"We'll have them to dinner," Marcelo said positively. "You can see her then."

Her father finished his Bloody Mary and yelled at the waiter to bring him another.

On Monday morning she was in the classroom with her students. She loved teaching, and she loved her students. They were around eight years old, which she believed was the best age for children. They were no longer babies, and they weren't close to being teenagers. They were at a stage in their lives where they could safely be open to the world. Of course some of them had disabilities, and some of them had already had bad experiences, but they didn't have the heavy baggage that they would have by high school. And generally they were so delightful that Sara felt blessed to teach them.

Being a third grade teacher, she had to cover a range of subjects including religion, mathematics, reading, writing, spelling, science, and social studies. Her day was divided into segments according to subject, the content was established for her, and the text books were selected for her. But that still left a lot of room for her individual personality, and she found that she could be creative within the limits of the curriculum. She understood that her students needed and actually appreciated structure.

Third grade was a special year for her students since during that year they prepared for their first Holy Communion. Sara wasn't directly involved in that process, though she supported it with her segment on religion, and she answered their questions on issues that might not have been explained clearly to them by Sister Helena, who had direct responsibility for preparing them. You never knew what questions they would ask, so they kept you on your toes.

For today she had assigned a children's version of the story of Abraham and Sarah, which was one of the selected readings from the Old Testament. She had them read the story aloud, letting each of them read a sentence or two.

"Once there was a man named Abram," Erin read.

"One day the Lord came to talk to Abram," Roberto read, "and Abram asked: 'Who will have all my things when I die?' "

"God promised Abram and his wife Sarai that one day they would be parents," Tamisha read, "even though they were old and had no children."

They continued reading through the part where the Lord decided to change Abram's name to Abraham, which means "father of many," and Sarai's name to "Sarah," which means "princess."

Jorge read the part where Sarah hears God tell her husband she would have a son.

"She started to laugh," Mary read, "but covered her mouth and laughed to herself because she didn't want to be heard. Then she said to herself: 'How can I have a child? I'm almost a hundred years old.' "

But a year later Sarah had a son, and they named him Isaac, which means "he laughs."

They thanked God for giving them Isaac.

"I like that story," Erin said.

"But wasn't Sarah too old to have a child?" Roberto asked.

"Without the grace of God she was," Sara said. "But with God's grace, all things are possible."

"Why did God change their names?" Jorge asked.

Mary raised her hand and waved it.

"Mary, why do you think God changed their names?"

"He wanted them to have the names they have in the Bible."

"That's right. And he wanted them to have names that had the right meaning. Remember when God said to Abram that he would have as many children as all the stars in the sky? Well, that's why God gave him a name that means 'father of many.' It fits him better than his old name."

"Could God change my name to 'George?' " Jorge asked.

"Of course He could. But so could you. Would you like us to call you 'George?' "

Jorge shrugged. "I don't know."

"Would you like to try it?"

Jorge nodded.

"If you change your mind, you can always go back to 'Jorge,' " Sara told him.

"When Sarah heard God tell her husband she would have a son," Tamisha said, "why did she laugh?"

"That's a good question. Why do you think?"

"If she was really a hundred years old, she must have thought God was kidding."

"Do you think God kids us?"

"My father kids me," Roberto said.

"What do you think, George?"

"If God feels like kidding us, why not?"

"Does anyone have another idea?"

Erin raised her hand.

"Erin, what do you think?"

"I think Sarah laughed because she was happy."

"How many of you think that's why she laughed?"

Almost all of the girls and two of the boys raised their hands.

"How many think she laughed because she thought God was kidding?"

Most of the boys raised their hands.

"Any other ideas?"

"Maybe she laughed because she was nervous," Tamisha said. "I laugh when I'm nervous."

"Maybe she laughed because she was surprised," Christina said.

"Those are all good explanations," Sara said.

"If it was you," Roberto asked her, "why would you laugh?"

Sara laughed. "For the same reason I laughed now."

"Why did you laugh now?"

"Because I feel blessed."

"So will you let us out early for recess?"

Sara laughed again. "We'll see."

While going to Fordham she lived at home and commuted, taking the subway from Woodlawn to Fordham Road and then a bus the rest of the way. She already had girlfriends there from St. Barnabas, including Regina, and she knew some boys, but the boys who made her a center of attention were new ones, mostly from Westchester and the Bronx but also from other parts of the country. Having attended a school for girls she wasn't used to being surrounded by boys, and it took her a while to stop them from distracting her. She eventually gained a reputation for being hard to get, which discouraged most boys from approaching her.

During her college years she had three boyfriends, all of them the same body type and mental type. They were lean and sinewy, not much taller than she was, and they were all intellectuals in one way or another. One was an aspiring actor, another was a poet, and another was a graduate student in history. At one point in her relationship with them she brought them home to meet her family, if only to satisfy her mother that she wasn't ignoring the opportunity that college offered girls to find husbands. Her father didn't think much of them since they were the complete opposite of him, and none of them was a Yankees fan, but her mother liked them all. In fact, her mother pushed her to accept a proposal of marriage from the graduate student, and when she turned him down her mother told her she might regret it.

"What I would regret," she told her mother, "is marrying a man I didn't want to spend my life with."

"Well, I think Gregory would have been a good man to spend your life with."

"He's a good man, but not for me to spend my life with."

"You mean you weren't in love with him."

"I was in love with him, but that doesn't mean I wanted to marry him."

"What *does* it mean?" her mother asked, looking worried.

"It doesn't mean I was sleeping with him either."

"Thank God for that. So what does it mean?"

"It just means I was in love with him."

"But you're not anymore."

"I still like him. And I hope we'll always be friends. But I don't want to marry him. I don't want to marry anyone yet."

"If you wait too long, the good ones will all be taken."

"I don't believe that. The men who marry young are doing it for the same reason as the women who marry young. They're afraid they won't find anyone better."

"Maybe they won't."

"If they don't have confidence in themselves, then I don't want to marry them. I mean, I don't want to marry a guy who's afraid he won't find anyone better."

"I understand," her mother finally said. "I held out for your father. I had many other opportunities, but I wouldn't settle for anything less."

"So don't worry. I know what I'm doing."

Sara graduated from Fordham with a degree in English, happy with her B average since she had met a lot of people and done a lot of things in college besides studying. She looked for a job with a newspaper, a magazine, or a book publishing company, but she found one with the head office of a retailer that had stores in every state. Though she was hired by the internal communications department, within six months she was working as the assistant to a woman who bought children's clothes, dealing with suppliers.

She was planning to get an apartment in the city as soon as she had saved enough to make a deposit on the rent, but her move from Woodlawn was accelerated by a notice on the bulletin board about an apartment to share in the East 80s. When she called the number she found that the person with the apartment to share didn't work for the retailer but for a bank, and that a friend had posted the notice.

They met for drinks that evening after work, and they got along immediately. Clara was from LaCrosse, Wisconsin, with a bachelor's in Spanish from the University of Wisconsin and a master's in international business from Thunderbird, which Sara had never heard of but assumed was a good place to go for that subject. Clara had done her junior year abroad in Spain, and she was in love with all things Spanish and Latin American.

Clara was vivacious and outgoing, not the kind of roommate who would mope around with nothing to do. She also had a sense of humor—when she laughed, her light blue eyes sparkled. Among her attractions, she offered a perspective that was far removed from the one Sara brought from Woodlawn. And to top it off, their names rimed: Clara and Sara.

The apartment had two bedrooms. The one that had been recently vacated by Clara's previous roommate, who had gotten married and moved to Atlanta, was on the street, and the other was on the airshaft. The previous roommate had left her furniture, so the room was ready to be occupied. But first they had to meet with the landlord. The apartment was under rent control, and if Clara moved out, the rights would pass to Sara as long as she was already on the lease.

Sara's parents were not happy about her moving to the city, though she had long prepared them for it. Her father had no use for the city, meaning Manhattan, and her mother said it was a waste of money to pay rent when she could live at home for free. What her mother really meant was that she didn't like the idea of Sara having the freedom as an unmarried woman to have a man in her bedroom. When they met her roommate they were reassured since Clara was a Catholic. At least they could assume that Clara wouldn't be a bad influence on their daughter, though of course they had no idea.

Clara had a boyfriend. His name was Alberto, he was from Colombia, and he was working on a doctorate in economics at New York University. They talked with each other frequently, but they saw each other only on weekends, which Clara spent at his apartment in the Village. That left Clara free to do things with Sara on weekday evenings, and since Clara was older and more experienced in the ways of the city, Sara happily let Clara lead the way.

They mostly went to art exhibits, concerts, dance events, and lectures that had to do with Spain or Latin America. They didn't go to plays in Spanish since Sara wouldn't have understood them, but she had taken Spanish in college, and being immersed in the culture, she was learning more and more of the language. Clara spoke Spanish perfectly, having spent a year in Spain living with a family that spoke no English, and Clara was always ready to explain the grammar and correct Sara's pronunciation. But they never reached the point where they spoke Spanish with each other, except when they had too much to drink.

On Wednesdays, at Clara's insistence, they went to bars where you could meet guys. Clara had met Alberto in such a bar, so she could give a testimonial. Of course she wasn't looking for another guy, but Sara wouldn't go alone to these places, so Clara accompanied her and helped her spot prospects while they sat at the bar and sipped white wine. If two guys asked them to go and have dinner with them, Clara on a nod from Sara would go along with them just to give Sara a chance to get to know the guy better. If things were going well, Clara always found a graceful way to bow out and leave Sara alone with the guy.

Early in their relationship Sara confided to her roommate that she was still a virgin. Clara didn't seem surprised, but she told Sara that if she was going to have sex she should start taking birth control pills.

"Do you take them?" Sara asked. They were in the bathroom,

where Clara was applying a magic cream to an almost invisible blemish on Sara's face.

"Of course I take them. I'm not ready to be a mother."

"But it's against our religion."

"It's against our religion to have sex with a guy before we're married. So if I'm damned for one, I might as well be damned for the other."

"Do you ever confess what you're doing?"

"I did once. I had a young priest, and he was embarrassed."

"What did he tell you?"

"He told me to stop doing it."

"Is that why you don't go to church anymore?"

"I don't go to church because I spend Sunday morning in bed with Alberto." Clara put the cover on the jar of cream and set it down. "But I still believe in God, and I know He'll forgive me for what I'm doing because I'm not harming anyone."

"Do you want to have children?"

"Oh, yes. I want to have a lot of children."

"So do I. My mother wanted to have more children, but she couldn't. I don't know why. She hasn't ever told me."

"Parents need to have their secrets. You wouldn't want to know everything about them."

"I can't imagine anything I wouldn't want to know about my mother."

"What about your father?"

"I'm sure there are things I wouldn't want to know about him. He's a ladies' man."

"I could tell that. As he shook my hand, he was peering down my blouse."

Sara laughed. "I didn't notice, but that's my father."

"My father checks out women too, but he's more discreet because he's a lawyer."

"When did you start taking the pill?"

"Right after I met Alberto."

"Why didn't you take it before?"

"I wasn't having sex with any of those other guys regularly. I was timing it. And I was relying on the grace of God."

"So you were taking a chance."

"I was. I could have gotten pregnant."

"What if you had?"

"I would have had the baby," Clara said without hesitation. "I wouldn't ever have an abortion. That's murder."

"But it's okay to kill sperm?"

"The pill doesn't kill sperm, it just makes them ineffective."

Sara absorbed this new information. "Did you ever make a guy use a condom?"

"I did with one guy. But that's not approved by the church either. So what would I gain?"

"Protection," Sara said.

"You mean against disease? Well, that's why I made that particular guy use a condom. I'd heard he slept around, and I didn't want to get whatever he might have."

"So why did you have sex with him?"

"That's a good question," Clara said. She reached inside the medicine cabinet and found a pair of tweezers. "You want an honest answer?"

Sara nodded, guessing what it was.

"I have no idea why I had sex with him. There are times when our minds and our bodies are in different worlds."

Sara's mind was in a different world from her body the first time she had sex with a guy. He was an actor, a waiter in a Spanish restaurant, and he was the sexiest guy she had ever seen in real life. As he served them dinner she couldn't take her eyes off his mouth. And two weeks later she was at his apartment, in bed with him.

That would have been a good time for Sara to start taking the pill, but she had qualms about it, so she timed her dates with the actor and relied on the grace of God.

The relationship, if you could call it that, only lasted about six months. The actor, who could have had almost any woman he wanted, found someone else, and Sara was surprised by how little it hurt to be dropped by him. She was also thankful for not getting pregnant.

After that affair her mind and her body were in the same world. She met a lot of guys, and she dated some of them, but she had sex with only two of them. The first guy was a copywriter for an advertising firm, and the second guy was a reporter for a newspaper. They were lean, sinewy, and intellectual—the type of guy she had always preferred. They had gone to good colleges, and they had good careers. In both cases she liked the guy, and she had some good times with him, but after a while she realized that she didn't want to spend her life with him, so she broke off relations and was thankful for not getting pregnant.

Now, as she left the school at the end of the day, she couldn't believe that she had been thankful for not getting pregnant. Of course it had occurred to her that her present predicament was a punishment for what she had done as a single girl. Or that it was the result of her having received her full quota of God's grace not to get pregnant, and there wasn't any more for her.

The voice of her mother said: "You see? You gambled away what God gave you. If you had only saved it for your husband, you wouldn't have a problem now."

"I *would* have a problem," she told her mother. "I have a disease."

"And where did you get it?"

"I didn't get it from anywhere. I was born with it."

"Oh, now you're trying to blame it on me."

"I'm not trying to blame it on you. I'm only pointing out that I didn't catch this disease from any of the guys I had sex with before I was married."

"That's what you think, but you don't know."

She was so involved in this conversation that she almost bumped into the young priest who was standing on the sidewalk in front of the church. Father Paul was from Ireland, and they said he might be one of the last to come from there since the

Irish economy was booming and boys now had a lot of other opportunities. Sara respected him as a priest but she also liked him as the younger brother she had always wanted.

Recovering, she said: "Hi, father."

"Hi, Sara. How was school today?" he asked in his soft brogue.

"School was great. The children were a joy as usual."

"You know, I've noticed that of all the teachers, you're the one who smiles the most and laughs the most."

"I feel blessed."

"Have you always felt blessed?"

"I have," she said. "But I was just wondering—when I almost bumped into you—is there any limit to God's grace?"

"What do you mean?"

"Well, is there some quota that after you've received it there isn't any more for you?"

Father Paul smiled. "That's the kind of question we get from a kid who's preparing for her first Holy Communion. You know the answer."

"I know what I was taught. There's no limit to God's grace."

"Then why did you ask the question?"

"I had a lapse. I always have a lapse when I talk with my mother."

"When were you talking with your mother?"

"Just now. She's a voice in my head," Sara explained when the priest began to look at her as if she were loony. "Don't we all have our mother's voice in our heads?"

"I guess we do," the priest said. "A moment ago I heard my mother telling me not to stand outside in this weather without a coat on."

Sara laughed. "So you understand."

"My mother also tells me to eat vegetables."

"Mine doesn't do that. She gave up trying to get us to eat vegetables. My sister and I would eat only meat and potatoes, just like our father."

"I saw your father earlier today. He was sweeping his walk."

"It didn't snow, did it?" she asked, looking around.

"No, he was just trying to clean up the remnants from the last snow."

"I'm going to his house now."

"Give him my blessing. And tell him he doesn't have to go all the way over to St. Barnabas. We have a perfectly good church here at St. Brigid."

"You tell him that."

"I already have. But you might have more influence on him."

"I have absolutely no influence on him," Sara said. "He does what he wants."

"I can see he does," Father Paul said. "In fact, he reminds me a bit of my father."

"Then maybe you can help me deal with him."

"Maybe I can. Just let me know when you need me."

"Thanks, father. And thanks for answering my question."

"I didn't answer your question. You did."

"I guess I did. And oh," she said before turning away from him, "you really shouldn't be standing outside in this weather without a coat on."

He grinned. "Thanks, mom."

She scheduled the surgery for the last Friday in January. She got a substitute teacher for only that day since Dr. Vesely had assured her that after resting over the weekend she would be able to resume teaching on Monday.

On Thursday after school Marcelo drove her to Columbia-Presbyterian Hospital and helped her check in. He stayed while she did the last pre-op testing and left her only when visiting hours were over. The procedure was scheduled for six the next morning, subject to any emergencies, and he told her he would be there then.

He arrived a few minutes before they transferred her from the bed to the gurney, and he walked with her to the holding area for the operating room, and he stood by her until they got the green light to bring her in.

He kissed her tenderly and said: "Don't worry. You have the best doctor in the city."

"I know. I love you."

"I love you too."

Before they put her out she blessed herself and asked God not to let anything happen to her, unnecessarily reminding Him that her husband and her father needed her. And also her students, who she hoped would have a good substitute.

FOUR

WHEN SHE OPENED her eyes, coming out of the depths, she saw Marcelo and Dr. Vesely standing at the foot of her bed. They were talking with each other.

"Hey," she said, letting them know she was awake.

Marcelo came and took her hand, asking: "How do you feel?"

"A little groggy, but other than that I feel fine."

"It went well," Dr. Vesely told her. "It took longer than I expected, but I got it all. Now, that might not solve the problem, so don't get your hopes up."

"I won't," Sara said, trying not to.

"Do you feel like eating?"

"Yeah. I'm starved." She hadn't eaten or drunk anything since the night before.

"I'll ask them to bring you some breakfast."

"You'll be home by noon," Marcelo said, still standing by the bed and holding her hand.

When the doctor had left them Sara asked: "Did she tell you anything she didn't tell me?"

"No. She wouldn't do that."

"I know she wouldn't. I guess I'm overanxious."

"It's understandable. You just had surgery."

She peered under the sheet and saw the bandage over her navel, where Dr. Vesely had gone into her with a laparoscopic instrument.

"How's the pain?" Marcelo asked.

"It's not too bad."

"They gave you something for it. But when it wears off, you may want more."

"I'll let you know, but right now I just want you."

"I just want you," Marcelo said, smiling at her.

"So it's enough that we have each other?"

"It's more than enough."

When the breakfast arrived she wolfed it down, and within an hour she had met the nurse's conditions for releasing her.

Marcelo brought the car from where he had parked it and helped her into it. He made sure that she was comfortable before he got in. And he drove carefully, avoiding every pothole and bump from Manhattan to Yonkers.

By the time they got home she was ready for a nap, and she slept through the afternoon.

For dinner he made her *pollo guisado,* or chicken stew, which he had learned to make from his mother. It was comfort food and guaranteed to make you feel better no matter what ailed you. And it did make her feel better.

As they were lingering at the table she said: "I forgot to ask her how long we have to wait before we try."

"She told me," Marcelo said. "You have to go through a period, and then we can try."

"Does she want us to keep using the syringe?"

"Yes. But that doesn't prevent us from doing it naturally."

"My father still thinks we only have to do what normal couples do, and we'll have a baby."

"I don't know what he thinks we do."

"My father has a big imagination about sex."

"Then he's like most men."

"I guess he is. But women also have a big imagination about sex. They just use it differently than men do."

"I don't have an opinion on that," Marcelo admitted. "I only know how I imagine having sex with you."

"You must imagine having sex with other women."

"I notice them, and I check them out. But my imagination doesn't go beyond the stage of arousal."

"Did it go beyond the stage of arousal when you met me?"

"Of course it did. It still does."

"Gracias," she said, reaching for his hand.

When they lay down in bed that night he drew her toward him and kissed her, saying: "Whatever happens, I love you more than *el mundo entero*."

"I know, and I love you the same way."

Before going to sleep she thanked God for giving her Marcelo and she prayed that her dream would come true.

When they went to her father's house on Sunday to drive him to church, he was waiting for them on the front porch.

"Where have you been?" he asked crossly as soon as Sara got out of the Honda.

"I told you. I had surgery on Friday."

"You never mentioned it."

"I know I did. I guess you weren't listening."

"I always listen. If you'd told me you were having surgery, I would have remembered."

"Well, anyway," she said, holding the door of the Crown Victoria open for him, "I had surgery on Friday, and I was recovering yesterday."

"I hope you didn't have a hysterorectomy," her father said, getting into the passenger seat.

"You mean hysterectomy." She closed the door and got into the back seat, and Marcelo started backing out of the driveway. "I didn't have one."

"They wanted your mother to have one."

"They did? I didn't know that." She remembered what Clara had said about parents needing to have their secrets. "Why did they want her to have a hysterectomy?"

"They said she had a problem."

"Do you remember what kind of problem?

"It was some kind of woman's problem."

"I didn't think it was some kind of man's problem."

"It wasn't. Women don't have our problems. They don't have to worry about their prostrates."

"You mean prostates," Sara said. "You don't have a problem with yours, do you?"

"Naw. The last time I saw my doctor he said I had the prostrate of a nineteen-year-old."

"How long ago was that?" Marcelo asked with his eyes on the road in front of him. "When you were nineteen?"

"Hah hah, you're funny," her father said. "As a matter of fact, it was less than a year ago."

"So you don't remember," Sara said, "what her problem was."

"Are you still talking about your mother? How would I remember? It was one of those long medical words that don't mean anything."

"By any chance, was it endometriosis?"

"That sounds familiar."

"Maybe it sounds familiar," Marcelo suggested, "because Sara mentioned it before."

"Why would Sara mention it?"

"Because she has it."

"She does? Who did she get it from?"

"She didn't get it from anyone. It's not transmitted sexually."

"It might be transmitted genetically," Sara said.

"There's evidence that it might be," Marcelo said. "If your mother had it, then you had a higher risk of having it. But there are a lot of other factors."

"I hope you're not blaming Sara's problem on her mother, God rest her soul."

"We're not blaming it on anyone," Sara said.

"Including Sara," Marcelo said.

"Well, I don't know what I did to deserve it," her father said. "I have two daughters, and neither of them has given me a grandson."

"Then why don't you start putting pressure on your other daughter," Marcelo said. "At least Sara is trying."

"How can I put pressure on Becky if I never see her?"

"Maybe that's why you never see her," Sara said. "She doesn't want the pressure."

"So if I don't put pressure on her, maybe I'll see her, but then she won't give me a grandson."

"You think that's the only reason why she would have a baby? To give you a grandson?"

"I can't think of any other reason."

"She might want one."

"She doesn't want one. She doesn't want a husband. But she has a husband. Do you know why?"

"No. I don't."

"Because you have a husband."

"I don't believe that."

"Then you don't know your sister."

Sara reflected. "Are you suggesting that if I had a baby, then Becky would have one?"

"For someone who has a master's degree," her father told her husband, "your wife can be slow on the uptake."

"She doesn't jump to conclusions about people," Marcelo said. "And that's good."

"Then if I don't have a baby, Becky won't have one?"

"Why would she? She doesn't want one."

Sara was silent, not wanting to believe what her father was saying about her sister.

"So I'm counting on you. If you don't have a baby, then I won't have any grandsons."

"Or granddaughters," Marcelo said.

"I think I just felt the pressure increase," Sara said.

"But there's another possibility," Marcelo said, waiting for a light to change. "If Sara can't have a baby, then maybe Becky will have one just to show her up."

"I never thought of that," her father said. "You mean like she had to have better grades and a bigger husband."

"You can't assume her husband's bigger," Marcelo said, playing the male game.

Her father chuckled. "I guess I can't. In fact, if it's true what they say about you colored guys—"

Sara was mortified, but she knew enough to let her husband handle the situation.

"It *is* true," Marcelo said as if it was a scientific fact. "Per pound of body weight we're three times bigger than white guys."

"Then I stand corrected. She doesn't have a bigger husband."

"Are you suggesting," Sara asked them, "that my sister would have a baby just because I couldn't have one?"

"That's what we're suggesting," Marcelo said.

"Well, I don't believe it. No matter how much of a pain in the ass my sister can be, she would never do a thing like that."

"You don't know your sister," her father said. "You could have made that light."

"I didn't want to push it," Marcelo said. "There could be a cop around."

"Oh, I get it. You don't want any trouble with immigration."

"That's right. I don't want them to deport me."

She admired Marcelo, who was a U.S. citizen, for joking with her father about what must have been a sensitive issue. And she had learned not to jump to her husband's defense in these situations, at least not when he was present. Since he didn't need her to defend him, she didn't feel the need to defend him.

Three years after Sara moved into the apartment Clara got the assignment she had always dreamed of—a position at the bank's branch in Bogotá, Colombia. After making her wait all those years the bank gave her only six weeks to pack her things and complete the papers and get settled in Bogotá and start working. Luckily, she got help from Alberto, whose family lived there. He couldn't move there with her at the time since he still needed another year to finish and defend his dissertation, but her being there gave him a reason to move at a somewhat faster pace toward completing his doctorate.

With his assistance Sara organized a party to celebrate her roommate's promotion. Alberto was in charge of inviting people, and Sara was in charge of food and drink. It was a great party. The food included a pile of *arepas* that one of the girls had made herself, and a case of *chicha* that was said to have been smuggled into the country right under the noses of the customs officials.

Evidently, they were so fixated on finding drugs in luggage that they ignored this potently alcoholic beverage.

Sara and Alberto accompanied Clara to the airport to see her off, with Sara standing back while they said goodbye, and then he brought her back to the apartment, where she wandered around missing her roommate but also being happy for her.

Over the next two years she had a succession of roommates who moved out to live with their boyfriends. When the last one moved out Sara was making enough money to pay the full rent, so she could afford to be picky in finding her next roommate. She posted a notice on the bulletin board, and she met several candidates, but she put off making a decision because her mother wanted her to share the apartment with her sister. She wasn't enthusiastic about the idea, not wanting to assume this kind of responsibility for her sister and not wanting to give her mother a way of closely monitoring her activities. But she had a good reason for turning people down since they would understand if she gave priority to her sister.

Inevitably, her feeling of responsibility outweighed her fear of having a spy in the apartment, and six months after her last roommate moved out, her sister moved in.

Becky had just completed a master's degree in finance from Fordham. As an undergraduate student majoring in mathematics, she had been a straight-A student, summa cum laude, and phi beta kappa, and as a graduate student she had received the highest honors. Becky had never lived away from home, and as far as Sara knew, she had never had a boyfriend. Not that Becky wasn't physically attractive, but there was something about her that put guys off. As one of Sara's boyfriends put it after meeting Becky, "She doesn't like guys, and guys can tell. In that respect, guys are like dogs."

That raised the question of whether Becky liked girls, but this didn't seem to be the case either. Becky had no girlfriends, and she rarely had anything good to say about girls. So you had to conclude that Becky just didn't like people.

Sara, who liked people indiscriminately, couldn't understand why her sister didn't like people, especially after all the attention she had received. Her mother, her father, and Sara had showered Becky with attention, and so had all her teachers in school and college. They had recognized her accomplishments, they had praised her, and they had rewarded her. So she should have felt good about herself.

Regina, the psychologist, believed that if a child got too much attention she would never develop her own sense of self-esteem. She became dependent on the attention, and if her parents stopped giving it to her she had nothing to fall back on.

Sara didn't quite believe this, but she did believe that if you didn't like yourself, then you couldn't like other people. And Becky evidently didn't like herself.

Though Becky had a master's degree, with an excellent transcript, she had trouble finding a job. She interviewed with a number of commercial banks, but she didn't get any offers. Sara, who by now had experience interviewing people, coached her on projecting a positive image, but she could feel Becky resisting her. Becky acted as if the last thing she wanted was to owe Sara for helping her get a job.

One night they discussed the situation while having dinner in a bar that Sara frequented. They were waiting for their food to arrive when Becky said: "I identified the problem. You know why I haven't been offered a job?"

"No," Sara said. "Why?"

"I don't want to work for a commercial bank. And they can tell."

"If you don't want to work for a commercial bank, then why have you been interviewing with them?"

"I don't know. I thought I wanted to work for a commercial bank, but the more I learned about what they do, the less I wanted to work for them."

"Then you need to think about what you *do* want to do."

"I don't need to think about it. I know what I want to do. I want to make a lot of money."

"You could make a lot of money," Sara suggested, "working for an investment bank."

"I've just begun to realize that."

"So line up interviews with investment banks."

"I intend to," Becky said with determination. "I think they're a much better fit for me."

Becky got a job with Silverman, a leading investment bank, and she was assigned to a department responsible for developing new products. She worked long hours and often didn't get home until after nine in the evening. She also brought work home on weekends, which was something Sara had never done. So she didn't have much of a social life.

At least once a week Sara took her sister out to dinner, and she introduced her to the bars where she could meet men, as Clara had done for her, but after going to several of them Becky said that she didn't want to go to those "meat markets." Sara had exposed her sister only to the most upscale bars, and she wondered what Becky would have thought of the other bars.

Becky went home every Sunday. Sara, who had been going home about once a month, felt obligated to accompany her. They took the subway to the Woodlawn stop and walked from there, arriving in time to go with their parents to the noon mass. At the Sunday dinner Becky dominated the conversation, telling their parents how well she was doing at her job and how much she was going to get as a bonus. Sara listened politely, feeling no compulsion to tell her parents how well *she* was doing at her job. In fact, she had just been promoted to buyer, but she felt it would have been competitive to tell her parents in front of Becky. So she told her mother over the phone since she knew it would make her parents happy.

A few weeks before Becky moved into the apartment Sara had started going to an exercise class two or three times a week, depending on her social engagements. She liked the classes, which combined yoga and stretching exercises for dancers. There were no machines and no aerobic exercises, but an emphasis on strengthening the muscles in your abdomen through a carefully designed series of exercises that included roll-ups, sit-ups, and leg-lifts. Within a few months she saw the difference in her body, and she began to feel tall and trim and healthy.

She also liked being in a room with women in their leotards or sweat clothes, with no men to distract them, so she didn't welcome the sight of a man who came for a trial class in October. She felt that he had invaded their privacy, and she hoped he wouldn't like the class.

He put his mat in front of her, and looking at his back in a Yankees tee-shirt she began to feel differently. He was lean and sinewy, with skin the color of the *café con leche* that Clara used to make for her. When he turned his head in the neck rolls she saw his profile, which matched an ideal in her mind, and something clicked inside of her.

They happened to leave the building together, and after a silent ride in the elevator during which she pretended to ignore him, he held the door for her and asked: "Do you mind if I ask you a question?"

"No," she said, stopping in the lobby.

"How long have you been taking these classes?"

Facing him, she noticed that along with the strong profile he had sensitive brown eyes. "About four months."

"Do they help you?"

"Oh, yeah." She couldn't talk about how they had improved her body, so she said: "They make me feel good."

"You mean instead of bad?"

At that point she knew he was interested in her, and that his question about the classes had only been an opening. "I mean healthy. I never feel bad."

"Never? I envy you."

"Well, almost never. I only feel bad when I hurt someone."

After surveying her face he said: "I bet that doesn't happen very often."

"It doesn't. But it does happen."

"I'm Marcelo," he said, extending his hand.

"I'm Sara," she said, taking it.

"Are you free to have a drink with me?"

"No. I promised my sister I'd take her out to dinner."

"You could still take her out if you had one drink with me."

She sized him up. "Do you mind if I ask *you* a question?"

"No," he said, looking at her directly.

"Did you take that class so you could meet women?"

"I didn't know it would be all women. And I certainly didn't know I would meet a woman like you."

From his looks and his accent she had guessed he was Latino, and she knew about *piropos*, the flattering comments Latinos made about women. But it still felt good, coming from him and not from a random guy on the street. She followed her instinct and said: "Okay. But I can only have one drink."

"I understand."

They headed toward Second Avenue, where they would have no trouble finding a bar.

"Do you work around here?" Marcelo asked.

"No. I work over on Sixth Avenue." She told him the name of the company.

"Really? I've been to your store in White Plains."

"Are you from Westchester?"

"No, I'm from the Bronx. But I take my mother to White Plains shopping."

"You're from the Bronx?"

"Yeah, I was raised there."

"What neighborhood?"

"Belmont. It's south of Fordham University."

"I'm also from the Bronx. I'm a BIC."

"What's a BIC?"

"A Bronx Irish Catholic."

"Then I'm a BDC."

It took her a moment to figure that out. "A Bronx Dominican Catholic?"

"That's right."

They had come to Second Avenue, where there was a bar on the corner. Sara had been there, but she hadn't taken her sister there since it wasn't upscale enough.

"Is this okay?" he asked, stopping.

"Sure," she said, having no problem.

Inside, he said: "Since we're only having one drink, would you mind sitting at the bar?"

"No, not at all." She had spent a lot of evenings sitting at bars, usually with roommates but also with guys who took her to the bars where they had met her.

"What would you like?" he asked her when they were seated.

"I'll have a Corona," she said, knowing they had it.

He ordered two of them.

"I'm thirsty from the exercise class," she explained. She didn't add that she had sweated pints of water, as she always did. She wasn't like the women who could go through a class without sweating or disturbing their hair.

"She gives you a good workout," he said, referring to the instructor.

"Yeah. She's good. She's a dancer."

"I could tell. She moves like a dancer."

Since most guys didn't have a clue about dancers, she noted this remark, conscious of the fact that if a guy had heard it he would have wondered if Marcelo was gay. It had crossed her mind seeing him in an exercise class with women.

When the bottles arrived she removed the wedge of lime from the neck of hers and took a swig of beer. As she watched Marcelo take a swig she remembered how her father had said Corona was a beer for women. She figured that Marcelo was in his late twenties or early thirties, and she had noticed right away that he didn't wear a wedding band.

"Where do you work?" she finally asked him.

"At New York Hospital."

It was only a few blocks east of there, which explained why he had gone to that exercise studio. "What do you do there?"

"I attend patients in the emergency room."

"Are you a doctor?"

"Yes. I am."

She had briefly dated a doctor, an orthopedist who was building a practice in sports medicine. At heart he was a jock and not her type. "What's your specialty?"

"Emergency medicine, but I plan to go into family medicine. I want to work at a clinic in the Bronx."

"You don't want to have a private practice?"

He shook his head. "I'm not doing it for money. I'm doing it to help people."

She had heard a lot of lines, but she could tell that what he had just told her wasn't a line, it was sincere. And she was touched. "I think that's wonderful."

He shrugged and said: "It's only what I've been called to do."

She stayed for a second drink, switching to white wine. She could have stayed longer since she really hadn't promised to take her sister out to dinner, she had just used that as an excuse for not jumping at his invitation. But now, unless she admitted that it wasn't true, she couldn't stay for a third drink, as much as she would have liked to.

Before they parted in front of the bar he asked for her phone number, and she gave him her business card, which he examined as if it were the key to her heart.

When she had recovered from the surgery, they resumed trying to have a baby, doing what normal couples did as well as using the syringe at Dr. Vesely's office. She checked her temperature twice a day to determine the optimal time for conception, and she was heartened by a spike in early April that indicated that she might be pregnant, only to have her hopes dashed by the onset of her period.

Shortly after that disappointment Becky and Bart came to dinner. They brought her father, along with several bottles of expensive wine. After working in a wine shop, Bart had started his own shop in Tribeca, financed by Becky, and he had become an expert on wine. He traveled regularly to France, Italy, Spain, and other wine-producing countries so that he could offer special wines to his clients, who included a number of celebrities. He refused to drink a bottle of wine that he sold for less than a hundred dollars, so the bottles of wine he brought tonight must have cost him fifty dollars.

As Sara watched him open a bottle of wine in the kitchen, using a device that he carried around in a leather case, she wondered what Becky saw in him. He was big and clumsy, with stooped shoulders and a beer belly. His head was far too small for his body, and his eyes bulged like those of a cartoon character whose name Sara couldn't remember. He had a sloppy mouth, and he always tried to kiss her on the lips, which she avoided by turning her head, repulsed by the thought of tasting his saliva.

At dinner as usual Becky dominated the conversation, telling their father how well she was doing at her job. She had been promoted to a higher position in her department, and now she had ten people working for her. Sara didn't feel the need to mention that in her last corporate job she had more than twice as many people working for her.

"I like your payella," her father told Marcelo, helping himself to another portion from the pan on the table.

"I made it for you," her husband said.

"You didn't put any chicken in it," Bart said.

"I never do. It's a *paella marinera.*"

"The restaurants always put chicken in it."

"They do if it's a *paella Valenciana,* but not in a *marinera.*"

"Well, I don't know about that," Bart drawled.

Marcelo refrained from agreeing with him. He was good at hiding his lack of respect for her brother-in-law.

Though Sara asked her to remain seated, Becky insisted on helping her clear the table and carry things into the kitchen. On the second trip she realized why.

"You know," Becky told her, stopping at the table on which they were putting the dishes, "I was worried that I had the same problem you have."

"What problem?" Sara asked, though she could guess what her sister meant.

"Not being able to have a baby."

"I thought you didn't want to have children."

"I don't," Becky said. "It would interfere with my career. And Bart doesn't want to have children, so I don't have any pressure to have them."

Evidently her sister didn't feel the pressure from their father.

"You said you were worried," Sara prompted her.

"I was. But I'm not anymore. I had myself tested. And if I wanted to have a baby, I could have one."

"That's good news. I'm happy for you."

"But of course I don't want to have a baby."

Containing herself, Sara didn't ask: "So why did you tell me you could have one?"

FIVE

"I'M THINKING about adopting," Regina said, looking at the menu. They were at Angelo's for their monthly lunch.

"You are?" Sara asked, surprised.

"Well, I'm going to be thirty-five in April, and I don't want to be too old to adopt."

"Is there a legal limit?"

"No. But imagine adopting a kid at fifty."

Sara considered. "I can't imagine doing that. But at forty, yes. That's not too old."

"If you're forty, you'll be sixty when your kid is twenty."

"I wouldn't have a problem with that."

"Your kid might have a problem with it," Regina said. "His friends would think you're his grandmother."

"Of course we're assuming we adopted babies."

"I wouldn't ever adopt a teenager. Not after seeing what my nephews are like."

"I was thinking of a child three or four years old."

"The older they are when you adopt them, the more problems you're going to have."

"You mean from the birth parents?"

"It's usually a single parent."

"So you want to adopt a baby."

"Yeah. I want to be its mother from the beginning."

"Where would you get it?" Sara asked, closing her menu. She had decided to order the lobster ravioli, a special for the day.

"Joe's mother would want to get it from Italy."

"Is that where Joe would want to get it?"

"He wouldn't argue with his mother."

"Are there babies available in Italy?"

65

"No. They're not having babies in Italy. Can you imagine? After all those paintings of *bambini* they did, Italians don't have babies anymore."

"I wonder why not."

"They want other things."

"You mean like designer clothes, and handbags, and shoes—"

"And vacations in Positano. Who knows? But they don't want babies."

"How do you know they don't want them? Maybe they have problems like we do."

"Maybe they do," Regina said, lighting a cigarette. "I never thought of that. But whatever the reason, there aren't any babies in Italy that we could adopt."

"Where else would you get one?"

"There are babies in China. They're all girls, but I'd actually rather have a girl."

"I would too. But I'm not particular."

"Joe is. He wants a boy."

"Then you better rule out China. They wouldn't ever let you have a boy."

"I thought of Africa, but Joe's parents would never accept it. They're as racist as the Southerners who fought integration."

"My father's a racist. He wouldn't accept our adopting a baby from Africa."

"Are you ladies ready to order?" the waiter asked, appearing out of nowhere.

"Yes, we are," Regina said. "I'll have the *bistecca*."

"How would you like it?"

"Medium rare. And a mixed green salad."

"I'll have the lobster ravioli," Sara said. "And a salad too."

"Would you like some more wine?" the waiter asked, eyeing their glasses.

"You can bring us a bottle of what we're drinking," Regina said, eyeing him.

"No problem," the waiter said with a slight bow.

When he had left them Regina said: "He's cute, isn't he."

"He's too young for you," Sara said, smiling.

"He should be in Italy making babies."

"If you can't get a baby from Italy, or China, or Africa, then where would you get one?"

"You should be able to guess where."

"You mean Latin America?"

"It's the logical place. They're still having a lot of babies, and they're not as dark as Africans so Joe's parents would probably accept it. Your father accepted your marrying Marcelo."

"He finally did, but it took a while."

"Well, it should be easier with a baby."

"It should be," Sara said. "People love babies no matter what color they are."

"So I could probably get a baby from Latin America," Regina said, exhaling smoke. "But I'd still have a problem. I wouldn't know what I was getting."

"You mean there could be something wrong with the baby."

"That could be why it's available. The mother could have been a drug addict or a lunatic. You never know."

"Wouldn't you check on the mother?"

"Yeah. But they're selling a baby. If you were selling your car, would you tell the buyer what's wrong with it?"

"That's not a good analogy."

"It's a perfect analogy. If they're willing to sell their baby for money, that's how they think."

"Then don't pay for it. Get it from a mother who wants a good home for her baby."

"That would be ideal," Regina agreed. "But we're dealing with the real world."

Sara looked for other possibilities. "What about a girl who has a baby by mistake and wants to put it up for adoption?"

"If that happens, she has an abortion."

"Not if she's a good Catholic."

"If she's a good Catholic," Regina said, "she's not having sex before she's married."

"Are you saying we weren't good Catholics?"

"We weren't at the time."

"Well, there could be a girl who lapses."

"Yeah, there could be," Regina said, flicking an ash off her cigarette. "But if I adopt her unwanted baby, I still don't know what I'm getting."

"You don't know what you're getting if you have your *own* baby. I mean, you could have a defective gene. Your husband could have a defective gene."

"He does. He likes football. Okay, you're right. You never know what you're getting. But if it was your own baby, you'd love it no matter what was wrong with it."

"I guess you would." Since it was Sara's turn to make a joke, she added: "Your mother loves you."

Laughing, Regina blew smoke at her. "Well, I'm not ready to adopt yet. We're still trying to have our own baby. How are things going with you?"

"We're still trying. We're still praying for a miracle."

"If anyone deserves one, you do."

Their salad arrived, and as they were eating it Sara said: "I need your opinion on something."

"Sure. What is it?"

"My sister got tested. I mean, to see if she could have a baby."

"She did?" Regina said, looking up from her plate. "And what did they find?"

"They found that she could have a baby."

"So she doesn't have the problem you have?"

"No. She doesn't have any problem."

"Well, lucky for her."

"Yeah. Lucky for her."

"Does she want to have a baby?"

"She claims she doesn't."

"Then why did she get tested?"

"That's what I need your opinion on. Why do you think my sister got tested?"

"To prove she could do something you can't do."

"That's what I thought," Sara said. "But I feel bad having such thoughts about her."

"Don't feel bad," Regina told her. "That's how your sister is. She's always trying to show you up."

"I know she is. But why does she feel she has to? What did I ever do to her?"

"You didn't do anything to her. It's what you are that she can't stand. You're a good person, a loving person. You've never had a mean thought in your life."

"I'm having a mean thought now about my sister."

"It's not a mean thought. It's an explanation for why your sister got tested."

"How do you know it's the right explanation?"

"Your sister told you about the test. If she hadn't wanted to show you up, she wouldn't have told you. She would have kept it to herself."

"Well, maybe she wanted to show me up, but I don't believe she wanted to hurt me."

"Why else would she have told you she could have a baby?"

"I don't know. And it did hurt me. When I told Marcelo about it he could tell how much it hurt me."

"Did he agree with me about why she did it?"

"Oh, yeah. But he said I should forgive her. I should realize how unhappy she is."

"Have you forgiven her?"

"I think I have. It was only words, it wasn't a deed."

"The test was a deed."

"But she didn't *do* anything to me."

"I guess she didn't. At least this time she didn't break your dolls or trash your yearbook."

"And it has no effect on whether I can have a baby," Sara said, thinking positively. "It proves she can, but it doesn't prove I can't."

"It actually doesn't prove anything," Regina said, setting her fork down on the salad plate. "The test could be wrong."

Marcelo didn't wait until Wednesday, when he could have seen her at exercise class. He called her at work on Tuesday and invited her to dinner that evening.

Sara accepted and agreed to meet him at a Spanish restaurant on York Avenue where she had gone many times with Clara. As she entered the restaurant and inhaled the aroma of saffron, onions, and pimiento she realized how Clara, with her love of all things Spanish and Latin American, had unwittingly prepared her for Marcelo.

He was standing at the bar, and he greeted her by taking her hand and kissing her lightly on the cheek.

From always being greeted this way by Clara's friends, she understood that the kiss was a formality, but she felt it was more than just that. And when he put his hand on her back to guide her to a table, she went along gladly.

"You said you'd been here before," he said when they had sat down at the table.

"I used to come here with a former roommate. This was her favorite Spanish restaurant."

"A former roommate? Where is she now?"

"The bank she works for sent her to Colombia."

"I assume she speaks Spanish."

"She speaks it fluently. And she taught me some phrases."

"So you understand Spanish."

"At least I can understand the menu."

"What do you like here?"

"I like the fish," Sara said, "especially the *merluza a la Vasca*. I also like the *paella*."

"I can make *paella*."

"Is that an invitation?"

He smiled. "Yes. It's an open invitation."

Responding to the offer in his eyes, she imagined accepting it, but she only said: "Thanks. I'll keep it in mind."

At that point a waiter came to take their drink orders.

"I'll have a glass of white wine," she told him.

"I could order a bottle of good Spanish wine," Marcelo said.

"All right. But we're splitting the check."

"I thought we were on a date."

"No. We're only having dinner together. And until now we've only had a drink together."

"Two drinks."

"But that's all."

He ordered a bottle of verdejo.

When the waiter had left them, Marcelo asked: "Did you have a good time with your sister?"

"I always have a good time with my sister." She stopped, reconsidered, and then said: "The truth is, I didn't have dinner with her."

"I know you didn't."

"How did you know?"

"I could tell. And I knew what you were doing. When a guy you meet in exercise class asks if you're free to have a drink with him, you're not going to say you're free. You're going to say you have an engagement."

"But it didn't discourage you."

"It would have discouraged me if you'd said you were having dinner with your boyfriend. But dinner with your sister? You left the door open."

"I meant to," she admitted.

"Do you have a sister?"

"Yeah. I do. And I never have a good time with her."

"Never? Why not?"

"My sister is an unhappy person."

He nodded as if he could understand. "And being around her makes you unhappy."

"It does," she said. "And I feel like it's somehow my fault that she's unhappy."

"I assume she's younger."

"Four years younger."

"Do you have any other brothers or sisters?"

"No. There's just the two of us."

"Are your parents alive?"

"They're both alive."

"You're lucky," he said. "I wish my father was still alive."

"What happened to him?"

"He died of a heart attack. He was a bus driver."

"Does your mother still live in the Bronx?"

"Yes. In the same apartment."

"Do you have brothers or sisters?"

"I have two brothers and two sisters. I'm the oldest."

"That's one thing we have in common."

"We have other things in common."

"We do? Like what?" she asked.

"We both like *paella.*"

"That's true."

The waiter brought the wine and poured some for Marcelo. He tasted it, and then he nodded, indicating that it was fine. After pouring a half glass for each of them, the waiter asked if they were ready to order.

"We need a few more minutes," Marcelo told him.

The waiter obligingly left them.

"We were talking about your sister," Marcelo resumed as if for some reason he didn't want to drop this subject. "Where does she live?"

"She lives with me."

"You share an apartment with your sister?"

"I didn't want to, but my last roommate had moved out to live with her boyfriend, so her bedroom was available."

"If you didn't want to share your apartment with your sister, why did you do it?"

"My mother wanted me to do it."

"You always do what your mother wants?"

"No. But in this situation—"

"You felt responsible for your sister."

"How did you guess?"

"I feel responsible for my brothers and sisters, especially since our father died."

"Then we do have other things in common."

"I told you we did."

They had dinner together on Friday, and then again the following Wednesday. They went to another Spanish restaurant and a Cuban restaurant, both of which she had gone to with Clara, prompting Marcelo to ask if there was a Spanish or Latin American restaurant in New York that she hadn't gone to. She told him she had never gone to a Dominican restaurant, so he took her to a restaurant in Washington Heights, where they had *sancocho*.

When he greeted her and said goodnight to her, leaving her at the door of her building, he always kissed her on the cheek. And she began to wonder if he would ever kiss her on the mouth. But she didn't take the lead.

Then one evening he reminded her of his invitation for *paella*. Instead of going out on a Saturday night, they could have dinner at his apartment. By then she knew he lived in the East 70s, within walking distance of where she lived, and by then, having kept it in mind, she was ready to accept the invitation.

She arrived at seven, bringing olives and cheese she had bought at Balducci's. He greeted her with the usual kiss on the cheek and then he helped her remove her coat, which he hung in a closet. Evidently, the apartment had one bedroom, and it wasn't being shared.

He led her into the kitchen, where she saw a *paella* on the stove. It wasn't cooking yet, but already she could smell the saffron, onions, and pimiento.

"It's all ready," he told her. "I just have to turn on the stove. When would you like to eat?"

"Oh, I don't know. Around eight-thirty."

"Then I'll wait until seven-thirty."

"Do you have a dish for the olives?"

"Yes." He opened a cabinet, revealing a whole collection of dishes. He reached up and got a dish and handed it to her.

While she put the olives in the dish he opened a bottle of red wine. She had learned about Spanish wines from Clara, so she knew it was customary to drink red wine with *paella* even though it was essentially a seafood dish.

"Here," he said, handing her a glass of wine. "Try it."

She tasted the wine. She didn't like heavy red wines, but this one was light. She said: "I like it."

"It's tempranillo, a Spanish grape."

"It tastes familiar. I must have had it with Clara."

"Well, the Spanish make excellent wines, but they don't make a beer like Presidente." He had introduced her to Presidente in Washington Heights.

"I never had a Spanish beer."

"You haven't missed anything."

She carried the dish of olives, and he carried the platter of cheese into the living room, where they sat on the sofa and relaxed. In the background there was music from a Spanish radio station, a slow romantic song that she recognized as a *bolero*.

The wine went down smoothly, and before long they were on their second glass. Marcelo had brought the bottle from the kitchen and set it on the coffee table.

They were sitting about a foot apart, and she was intensely aware of his physical presence, so when it finally happened she was primed to lean toward him and meet the kiss on the mouth that was coming.

They didn't relocate to the bedroom, they stayed on the sofa, and it was like what she had experienced that first time with the actor, only now she wasn't just having sex, she was making love, and her body, her mind, and her soul were engaged.

It was after ten when, after burning a lot of energy, they ate the *paella*. There were only a few grains of rice left in the pan.

She was driving south on Broadway after stopping at the Korean grocer when she saw an old woman hobbling along, carrying a sign. It was on the long stretch of road between St. Cabrini and the junction with Warburton Avenue, where the Hastings police could always catch a driver for speeding.

Since the woman was old and looked as if she was in pain, Sara stopped and rolled down the window on the passenger side and asked: "Can I give you a ride?"

The woman halted and stared at Sara blankly as if she hadn't understood.

"Can I drive you somewhere?"

"Well, yes," the old woman said, "you can."

"Then hop in," Sara said, opening the passenger door. She realized that she could have used a better word since the woman was obviously incapable of hopping.

But the woman did manage to get into the car after putting her sign in the back seat.

"Where can I take you?" Sara asked her.

"Are you going as far as Yonkers?"

"Yeah. I live there."

"Well, if you can drop me off in front of St. Brigid, that would be fine."

"I'm going right by there."

"Thank you so much."

As she pulled out into the lane of traffic Sara asked: "Were you going to walk all that way?"

"If I had to, I was. I waited for the bus, and it never came."

"They don't run that often on Saturdays."

"I should have known that."

"Where did you come from?"

"Dobbs Ferry."

"Then you already walked a long way."

"I walked from the women's clinic."

"Were you demonstrating there?"

"I was standing there and holding up my sign."

"I gather you haven't been there regularly."

"I haven't. How did you guess?"

"If you had," Sara said, "you would have known the bus schedule."

"It was actually my first time," the woman said as they stopped for the light at Warburton.

"What made you decide to start demonstrating?"

"My grand-daughter had an abortion there."

"Your grand-daughter? How old is she?"

"She's sixteen. I told her she should have the baby and give it up for adoption, but she wouldn't listen to me."

"Did her parents tell her she should have the baby?"

"We all told her she should have the baby. We're Catholics. We're against abortion."

"I understand," Sara said. She imagined the girl having the baby and giving it up for adoption. That would have been perfect for Regina.

"She went to that clinic to find out what her options were. And of course they pushed the abortion. They do it for money."

"I guess they do."

"That clinic is a business like everything else, except that they make money by committing murder. They're just as bad as those contract killers."

"Well, maybe they believe they're helping people," Sara said, not wanting to judge them so harshly.

"Maybe they do," the woman said. "But that doesn't justify what they're doing. I'm sure the contract killers believe they're helping people."

"How's your grand-daughter?"

"She's all right physically. But now she's sorry. Now she wishes she'd had the baby."

So did Sara. It would have been good for everyone, except the owner of the clinic. And with that perception a specific grievance against the clinic was planted in her.

When they went to her father's house on Sunday to take him to church, he didn't come out to meet them as he always did. She rang the doorbell and waited for a while, then rang it again and waited again. And then she tried the outer door.

"This door is locked," she told her husband, who was standing by her father's car.

"He always locks it," Marcelo said.

"But he's not answering."

"Well, he couldn't be asleep at this hour." Marcelo knew that her father got up at five in the morning, no matter what.

"There's something wrong."

Marcelo joined her on the porch and pounded on the outer door. They had a key for the inner door, but the outer door couldn't be opened with a key. You could only unlock it from the inside, so at least they knew her father was there.

"I'll go around and try the back door," Marcelo said. He literally ran around the house and back and reported that it was the same situation.

With a key they unlocked the garage door and found a sledge hammer.

Before swinging at the outer door, Marcelo said: "If there's nothing wrong, he's going to kill me for wrecking his door."

"There's something wrong," Sara repeated. "Go ahead."

The door had no window, so he had to make a hole that he could put his hand through and get at the lock from the inside. Worried as she was, she couldn't help admiring the forceful way he swung the hammer. "You could have been a fireman."

"I could have," he said, opening the door.

By instinct she went straight to the kitchen, where she found her father lying on the floor. He was sprawled at the foot of a step ladder which he must have been using to change the bulb in the overhead light. He wasn't conscious.

Marcelo was right behind her, and she thanked God that he was a doctor.

"I feel a heartbeat," Marcelo said after putting the fingertips of a hand against her father's neck. "And he's breathing regularly."

"I wonder how long he's been lying there."

"A long time. I think he's hypothermic."

To save on his Con Edison bill her father always turned the heat down at night, and quickly checking the thermostat in the living room, she found that he hadn't turned it up to the level where he kept it during the day. So he must have been lying on the kitchen floor all night.

On her way back to the kitchen she heard Marcelo calling the paramedics. When he had hung up the phone he said: "He broke his leg."

"Falling from the ladder?"

"It looks that way."

"Well, that explains why he didn't call for help. He couldn't get up off the floor."

"The fall could have knocked him unconscious. There's a bump on the back of his head."

Knowing what her father needed, Sara hurried upstairs and got a blanket, which she laid over him gently.

"You could have been a nurse," Marcelo said.

"A fireman and a nurse," Sara said, smiling. "We would have made a great couple."

At that moment they heard the steps of heavy men in the front hall.

"We're in the kitchen," she yelled at them.

Two big guys with a stretcher appeared in the doorway.

Her father opened his eyes and asked: "Who the hell are they? And what the hell are they doing in my house?"

"They're paramedics," Marcelo said.

"Well, I don't need them. Help me get up, and I'll be fine."

"You have a broken leg and probably a concussion."

"You don't know what you're talking about."

"Don't you feel a pain in your leg?" Sara asked.

"I don't feel anything in my leg."

"It's numb from the shock," Marcelo said. He knelt down and told her father: "We have to get you to the hospital."

"I'm not going to any damned hospital."

"You have to," Sara said.

"They have to do X-rays and set your leg," Marcelo said.

"Just help me get up, and I'll be fine."

Marcelo signaled the two men, who tried to ease her father onto the stretcher. But he resisted, and they were stymied.

Then a woman in uniform, a pretty young woman with blond hair, appeared in the doorway and asked the men: "You guys need help?"

"Yeah, we do," one of them said. "He's not cooperating."

"Who are you?" her father asked, brightening.

"I'm Kelly," the young woman said.

"Is that your first name or your last name?"

"It's my last name." The young woman approached her father. "Now, why don't you be a good boy and come with me."

"I'll go with you," her father said, "but not with them."

"We need to get you onto the stretcher."

Her father cooperated with her, and within a few minutes the two men were bearing him away, with Kelly going along with him, holding his hand.

"Always the ladies' man," Marcelo said with admiration.

"He wouldn't listen to you or me," Sara said in resignation. "But along comes a blond, and he'll do anything she says."

"St. Peter must have left open the gates of heaven," Marcelo said, beginning a standard *piropo*.

"Because an angel got out," Sara said, completing it.

They followed her father to the hospital.

SIX

HER FATHER WAS taken to the emergency room at St. John's Hospital, where they examined him, took him to radiology, and brought him back to a holding area. Sara and Marcelo sat in the waiting area, looking up expectantly whenever a doctor or a nurse appeared. From time to time an orderly wheeled a patient out of the emergency room and through a door. Among these patients Sara counted four women who were in labor.

"That could be you," her mother's voice said as a moaning woman went by.

"No, it couldn't. I can't get pregnant."

"You could have gotten pregnant earlier."

"You don't know that," Sara argued. "I could have been born with endometriosis."

"You weren't born with it. You developed it."

"Well, I must have been at risk for it. Did *you* have it?"

"No. I didn't. I had something else."

At that moment a doctor approached them. With his blond hair and pink cheeks he looked younger than Marcelo.

"Are you with Mr. Quinlan?" he asked Sara.

"Yes. I'm his daughter." She wondered how he had guessed. Her father had probably told him she was an Irish girl with a colored husband.

"I'm Dr. Hansen," the young man said, extending his hand.

Sara shook it. "This is my husband, Dr. Solís."

Marcelo rose from the plastic chair and respectfully shook Dr. Hansen's hand.

"How's my father?" Sara asked anxiously.

"Your father's fine," Dr. Hansen assured her. "He's complaining about everything. Is that his normal personality?"

"Oh, yes," she said, smiling.

"I should have said he's complaining about everything except the pain."

"He's very tough," Marcelo said.

"He began to tell me how he shot a Japanese soldier out of a tree at Guadalcanal. I'm not sure what that had to do with the situation, but it was a great story."

"Can we see him?" Sara asked.

"I'll take you to him. And then I'll explain the situation."

They followed the doctor into a room where her father was lying on a bed with his head propped up on a pillow.

"Where have you been?" he asked gruffly.

"We've been in the waiting area."

"I want to get out of here."

"You will when you're ready."

"I'm ready now."

"You have a broken fibula," Dr. Hansen explained to him. "You also have a problem with your knee."

"What happened to his knee?" Marcelo asked.

"He injured it. I mean, he injured it a long time ago, but by falling from the ladder he made it worse. I saw in the X-ray what looked like a small piece of shrapnel near the joint."

"It's from a Jap mortar," her father said. "The yellow sons of bitches."

"It's amazing he was able to walk with that knee," Dr. Hansen said. "The joint is shot, and the piece of shrapnel isn't helping."

"Will he need a replacement?" Marcelo asked.

"Well, we can't fix it, and he can't walk with the knee in that condition."

"You don't know what you're talking about," her father said. "You're just a pair of kids playing doctor. I want to see a real doctor."

"We'll get a second opinion," Sara told him.

"If I were you," Dr. Hansen said with a look of understanding, "I definitely would."

"I want to get out of here."

"We'll set the broken bone, and we'll put a cast on his leg, and we'll get him into a room for tonight. And tomorrow we'll have an orthopedist look at that knee."

"There's nothing wrong with my knee."

"I know. But we'll have him look at it anyway."

Dr. Hansen left them, and they stayed with her father until an orderly wheeled him away to have the broken bone set. To kill time and get some nourishment they walked over to the Dunkin' Donuts on Odell Terrace, where they lingered for an hour.

It was almost four in the afternoon when her father was finally settled in a room. It had a view of the river, and for now the other bed was empty.

"Are they going to keep me here tonight?" her father asked.

"They need to keep you here," Sara told him, "so they can examine your knee tomorrow."

"I don't want them messing with my knee."

"They won't mess with your knee," Marcelo said. "They'll only examine it."

"I heard that kid," her father said scornfully. "He wants to replace it with a piece of iron."

"They don't use iron."

"Whatever they use, I don't want a knee replacement."

"You want to walk, don't you?"

"I can walk fine."

"Dr. Hansen doesn't think you can."

"I don't give a damn what that kid thinks. He doesn't know anything. And you don't either," her father added, just to make sure that Marcelo knew where he stood in the hierarchy of people who knew things.

"We'll get a second opinion," Sara told her father again.

"You can get all the opinions you want. I'm not going to have a knee replacement."

"Don't worry," Marcelo said. "They won't do anything without your permission."

"You're goddamned right they won't. Now, if I have to stay here tonight, I want you to bring me some things from home."

"What things?" Sara asked.

"I need my razor. I need shaving cream. I need aftershave lotion. I need deodorant—" The list got longer and longer.

Sara found the small notebook she carried in her handbag, along with a pen, and she started taking dictation from her father, applying the shorthand skills she had learned when girls were expected to be secretaries.

When they got home she called Becky to let her know what had happened. The phone rang, and rang, and rang, but no one answered. Of course they didn't have an answering machine since they didn't like having to deal with messages. If you wanted to reach them, you had to keep calling until one of them, usually Bart, felt like answering.

Unwilling to play this game, Sara left a message at her sister's work number. At least by the next morning Becky would check for messages at that number.

After school the next day, as she was going to check her father's house, she ran into Father Paul. He was standing in front of the church without a coat, smoking a cigarette.

"I saw your father this morning," he told her.

"You did?" She was afraid her father had escaped from the hospital. "Where?"

"At St. John's. I was making the rounds."

Relieved, she asked: "Is that one of your duties?"

"It is. Visiting the sick and praying for them."

"Did you pray for my father?"

"I prayed for what he asked for."

"What did he ask for?"

"He asked for God to get him out of there," Father Paul said, smiling. "And he asked for God to knock some sense into those idiotic doctors."

"Idiotic? That doesn't sound like a word he would use."

"He actually used the word 'shithead'."

"That sounds more like him."

Father Paul took a long drag on his cigarette. "He said they told him that if he doesn't have a knee replacement, he won't be able to walk."

"That's what the doctor in the emergency room told him. But he's not an orthopedist."

"When I saw your father an orthopedist had already examined him, and that was his opinion."

"It was? Well, we'll get a second opinion."

"When they say you can't walk, they usually mean you can't walk without pain. They don't mean you can't walk at all."

"They don't? Then the alternative to a knee replacement is walking with pain?"

"Some people have a very high threshold for pain."

"I know my father does. You know," she said, "he always claimed he had a piece of shrapnel in his leg. And he did. They saw it in the X-rays. The doctor said that it was amazing he was able to walk with that knee."

"He must have been in pain."

"Well, maybe that explains why he's so grumpy."

"I think it's his personality," Father Paul said. "But pain would make him grumpier."

"Well, let's assume he could walk without a knee replacement. But could he drive a car?"

"Which of his legs has the bad knee?"

She thought for a moment. "The right leg."

"Then it would be very painful to drive. Stepping on the gas and slamming on the brake, it's a big strain on your right knee. It's more painful than walking."

"How do you know?"

"I injured my knee playing soccer."

"What did you do to it?"

"I tore the cartilage."

"Did you have surgery?"

"It cured itself. It was a small miracle."

"Have you ever witnessed a big miracle?"

"I never have. But if the doctors are right," Father Paul said, "we'll witness a big miracle if your father can walk."

"And if he can drive."

"But why does your father need to drive? You take him to church, and he can do his shopping on Palisade Avenue."

"He drives to Woodlawn every day."

"What does he do there?"

"He hangs out with his friends from the old neighborhood."

"Where do they hang out?"

"At Monahan's. It's the neighborhood bar."

"I didn't think it was the neighborhood church."

"For some of those men," Sara said, "it's more important than the church."

"But he could hang out with people here. We have an active senior citizens group."

"I can't imagine my father in a senior citizens group."

"Well, we have a neighborhood bar on Palisade."

"You mean Hogan's?"

"I think that's the name of it," Father Paul said cagily, letting her know that now and then he had a pint there.

"He went there once, and he didn't like it."

"Why didn't he like it?"

"He didn't see any people he knew. He only saw people my mother knew."

"Then I guess he wouldn't like our senior citizens group. They're probably people your mother knew."

"If they're from this parish, they are. And besides, they're probably all women."

"They're a few men," Father Paul said. "But I thought your father was a ladies' man."

"He is, but he doesn't like women his age. He likes women my age or younger."

"So your father's an old lecher."

"That's putting it mildly. But he only has lecherous thoughts. He doesn't ever do anything. He's always been faithful to my mother."

"Except in his imagination."

"We all commit sins in our imagination, don't we?"

"I do," Father Paul admitted. "So I don't judge your father."

"I don't either. I accept my father. Though at times," she added, "it's not easy."

"I can see how it's not. You're his daughter, his wife, and his mother. You're his private trinity."

"I'm not all that. But he does need me."

"Do you need him?"

"My friend who's a psychologist would say I do since I put up with him. But I don't think I need him. I only want to take care of him."

"Then you're fine," Father Paul said, dropping the butt of his cigarette on the sidewalk and stepping on it. "I'll concentrate my prayers on him."

"Thank you, father."

When she entered her house through the back door into the kitchen she saw from the blinking light on the answering machine that there was a message.

Becky had returned her call at ten after nine. She sounded as if she expected Sara to be at home then instead of at school. And she sounded panicky as she asked for their father's room number at the hospital, ignoring the fact that Sara had provided that information in her message.

Sara called her sister at work, and was told by a new secretary—the third or fourth new secretary in as many months—that Ms. Quinlan was in a meeting.

"I'm her sister," Sara said, assuming that the "meeting" was a screening device.

"I'll tell her you called. Does she have your number?"

"You mean she really *is* in a meeting?"

"She's always in meetings."

Sara gave the secretary the name of the hospital and the number of her father's room along with the suggestion that Ms. Quinlan go and see him after work.

It was almost nine that evening when Becky finally called from her office.

"How's daddy?" Becky asked.

"He's fine." Sara had spent a few long hours with her father hearing his complaints about the food, the service, the doctor, and the man they had moved into his room. The only things he hadn't complained about were pain and the nurses.

"If it's not too late to visit him, I can have Bart meet me at the Glenwood station."

"They won't let you in. The visiting hours are over at eight."

"Oh, damn. I was hoping I could see him. I have to go to London tomorrow."

"How long will you be there?"

"A week or so."

"Then try to call him."

"I did try. But he didn't answer."

"Well, try again tomorrow," Sara said, though she knew that her father was as unlikely as her sister to answer a phone.

The next Saturday she went for dinner at Marcelo's apartment. They had ended up there after their date on Wednesday, and they had used the bed.

"Oh, that smells good," she told him, referring to the aroma that filled the apartment.

"Tonight I'm cooking Dominican," he said after kissing her formally on the cheek. "It's fried chicken with rice and beans."

"*Pollo frito con arroz y habichuelas.*"

"Good. Only we would say *chicharrón de pollo.*"

"*Chicharrón,*" she repeated. "That's what makes it hard to learn Spanish. The different countries have different words for the same thing."

"It happens mostly with words for food."

"So you say I love you the same way in all countries?"

"*Sí. Te amo.*" The way he said it he wasn't just telling her how to say it.

"*Te amo también,*" she said the same way.

He kissed her on the mouth, not formally. They kissed with a growing likelihood that they wouldn't make it to the kitchen.

"Before we go further," he said, drawing back, "I have to tell you something."

With a pang of fear she almost said: "I don't want to hear it."

He looked her directly in the eye and said: "Technically, I'm married."

"You asshole!" she wanted to cry, but she only said: "What? What do you mean?"

"I'm married, but I never lived with my wife, and we never consummated our marriage."

"When did you marry her?"

"Two years ago."

"Then why haven't you gotten a divorce?"

"I don't want a divorce. I want an annulment. We were married in the church."

"So how do you get an annulment?"

"You go to the archdiocese and file for one."

"I think I should go," she said, turning from him. Among other reasons for not wanting to stay in his apartment, she didn't want him to see her cry.

"No, wait," he said, reaching out and touching her shoulder. "I'm sorry. I should have told you upfront, but if I *had* you wouldn't have gone out with me."

"You're damn right I wouldn't have gone out with you. I don't go out with married men."

"And we wouldn't have gotten to know each other."

"You mean we wouldn't have had sex."

"It wasn't just sex," he said softly. "At least it wasn't just sex for me."

"It wasn't just sex for me either." She couldn't hold back the tears any longer. "But why did you let me fall in love with you and then tell me you're married?"

"I'm not married in the usual sense."

"If you were married in a church you are. Whatever problem you had with your wife, you're still married in the eyes of God."

"I know. That's why I want an annulment."

"And it's not possible that you never lived with her."

"It *is* possible. We were separated a few hours after we left our wedding reception."

All this time they had been standing in the hallway, and now that she knew she wasn't going to leave before she heard the whole story, she said: "Can we sit down?"

"Oh, yes. I'm sorry. Can I get you something to drink?"

"No, thanks." She knew that when you needed a drink, as she did now, it wasn't a good time to have one. She went to the sofa, which offered the comfort of being a familiar place, and she sat down at one end, avoiding the middle.

Without a word he sat down at the other end, leaving a buffer zone between them.

"All right. What happened after your wedding reception?"

"We were in the car," Marcelo said, "on our way to the inn where we were going to spend our wedding night, when she told me she'd made a mistake."

Sara could see how it might be normal for a brand new bride to feel that way.

"She said she suddenly realized that if we had a baby, it could be black."

"She hadn't thought about that before?"

"Evidently not. We hadn't had sex, so maybe she had no reason to think about it."

"Why didn't you have sex?"

"She's a Catholic."

"So am I."

"Well, she believes it's a mortal sin to have sex before you're married."

"So do I. If I wanted to make you feel bad, I'd say you got me to commit a mortal sin under false pretenses."

"You don't want to make me feel bad, do you?"

"I'm not that way. You're lucky."

"I know I'm lucky." That was a time to move toward her and

offer his hand as a sign of peace, but he didn't budge. He stayed at his end of the sofa.

"Did it ever occur to you," Sara asked after reflecting, "that she didn't have sex with you before you were married because she was afraid of getting pregnant and having a black baby?"

"No. It didn't. But if that was already in her mind, then why did she marry me?"

"You're smart, you're handsome, and you're a doctor."

"So she thought that if she married me," Marcelo said as if he were trying to understand, "she could get over it?"

"Yeah, maybe. But it must have been in her mind all along. I mean, how could she just suddenly realize it?"

"I don't know." He paused for a while, staring at the coffee table. "Well, that's my story."

"I believe it, but a lot of girls wouldn't."

"I never told it to anyone before."

"You haven't dated anyone?"

"No. I was hurt. And I didn't want to get hurt again. In fact, I almost didn't ask you out."

"Do I remind you of her?"

"Oh, no. You don't look anything like her."

"Was she a nurse?"

"No, she was a lawyer."

"Where did you meet her?"

"I met her in a bar. Where else?"

"You didn't meet me in a bar. But you could have," she added, not wanting to pretend that meeting men in bars was beneath her.

"I'm glad I didn't meet you in a bar."

"Well, at least we had a different start. But I don't know where we go from here."

"We keep going," he suggested hopefully, looking to see how she would react.

"When I didn't know you were married," she said, "it wasn't a problem. But now that I know, it *is* a problem. I can't go out with a married man."

"You mean your mother wouldn't like it?"

"That's one issue. But it's not the only one. I mean, what if you never get an annulment?"

"I'll get an annulment," he assured her. "My advocate says I have a strong case."

"But it could take years."

"It won't take years. I've been working on it for almost two years, so it won't take much longer."

"And what will happen when you get it?"

"We'll get married," he said as if she should have known.

"How do you know you want to marry me? And how do I know I want to marry you? We met only two weeks ago."

"That's long enough to get to know someone."

"It's not long enough. We don't know anything about each other. I didn't even know you were married. And what if there's something you don't know about me?"

"There are a lot of things I don't know about you. But I know the main things."

"You do? What are they?"

"You think about other people," he said. "You're responsible. You're caring. And you wouldn't have a problem if you had a black baby."

"I never thought about having a black baby."

"But you thought about having babies, didn't you?"

"Oh, yeah. A lot. But now that you mention it," Sara said, "they weren't any particular color. They were babies. They were gifts from God."

"That's what I expected you to say. So I do know you."

"Let's talk about it over dinner."

"Are you going to stay?"

"Only for dinner."

"I understand."

"I have to keep my mind clear." She rose from the sofa and headed for the kitchen. "Now, what about the *chicharrón*?"

Sara and her roommates had shared secrets, things they wouldn't have told their mothers or their boyfriends, and out of habit she continued sharing secrets with her new roommate. When she got home the night that Marcelo dropped the bombshell on her, she told her sister about it, sitting on the bed in Becky's room.

"What a creep," her sister said. She had her knees raised under the covers and her arms wrapped around them. "If he was married, he should have told you upfront."

"I know he should have. But then I wouldn't have gone out with him."

"Why would you want to go out with him?"

"I like him. In fact, I love him."

"How could you love someone who lied to you?"

"He didn't lie to me," Sara insisted. "He just didn't tell me everything upfront."

"He just left out a minor detail?"

"It's not a minor detail, but it's not the whole story."

"The story is, he's cheating on his wife."

"If he hasn't ever lived with her, and hasn't ever consummated his marriage, I wouldn't call it cheating."

"What would you call it?"

"I'd call it dating."

Becky pulled her knees up further. "If he lied to you about being married, how do you know he's not lying to you about what happened to his wife?"

"What you mean?"

"I mean how do you know his wife didn't throw him out for cheating on her?"

"I don't know. But I don't believe it happened that way."

"You believe that a woman would marry a Latino and suddenly realize that if they had a baby, it could be black?"

"Yeah. I believe that."

"How dark is he?"

"The color of coffee with cream in it."

"Then he must have had a black ancestor."

"Of course he did. And I don't have a problem with that."

"Well, daddy will."

"I know he will."

"But that's not the issue. The issue is, he's using you."

"How is he using me?"

"If he's married, he's having an adulterous affair with you, and he probably has no intention of leaving his wife. And if he's not married, he made up a story so he has an excuse for not marrying you."

"But he's trying to get an annulment."

"How do you know?"

"I don't know. But I believe him."

"I still think he's using you."

She finally left her sister's room and went to bed, where she lay on her back with the tears streaming down both sides of her face. She didn't believe what Becky had said, but she no longer fully believed what Marcelo had said.

Two days later they released her father from the hospital. They had no further reason to keep him there since he refused to have a knee replacement.

Marcelo took the afternoon off and helped get him home. He left his car at her father's house, got her father's car, picked her up, and drove her to the hospital.

Her father was packed and ready to go, standing on crutches in the hallway outside his room.

"Where have you been?" he asked crossly.

"I told you we'd be here at three," she reminded him.

"You should have been here earlier."

Without explaining to her father that they had jobs and other responsibilities, she leaned down and picked up his overnight bag. "Is this everything?"

"It's everything you brought me."

"How are you doing on the crutches?" Marcelo asked.

"I'm doing fine." As if to prove it, her father started moving briskly down the hallway.

She waited with him at the main entrance of the hospital while Marcelo went to get the car.

"They have a lot of Indians at this place," her father said. "Where are they coming from?"

"I assume they're coming from India."

"Well, they should stay there. We don't need them."

"If we didn't need them, they wouldn't be here."

After a silence her father said: "That young priest from St. Brigid came to see me."

"He told me he'd seen you. Do you like him?"

"Yeah. He talks like a real Irishman. But he doesn't know a damn thing about baseball."

"It's not a major sport in Ireland."

"I don't know why they like soccer so much. It's just a lot of guys in shorts running around and kicking a ball and never doing anything with it."

"While you're in that cast, you might want to go to St. Brigid. You could walk there."

"I don't want to go to St. Brigid. I want to go to my church. And what the hell does the cast have to do with it? You drive me to church anyway."

"I thought you might want to be more independent."

"I'm independent. I don't need anyone."

At that moment Marcelo pulled up in the Crown Victoria. He got out and came around and opened a back door of the car.

Her father handed the crutches to her with one hand clamped onto the door frame.

"I'll help you," Marcelo offered.

"I don't need help."

They watched as her father, leading with his butt, maneuvered into the back seat.

"What should I do with the crutches?" she asked.

"Put them in the trunk," her father said. "I don't need them. You can give them to charity."

Marcelo took the crutches from her, and while he put them into the trunk she got into the passenger seat.

"I need more room," her father said. "I can't bend my leg with this damn cast."

She reached down and found the lever that enabled her to slide her seat forward.

"More, more," her father said as her space contracted and his expanded.

"It won't go any further," she said at the point where she was almost completely out of leg room. It was lucky she didn't have long legs.

When they got him settled at home in his lounge chair he began to give her a list of all the things he needed.

"Before we do that," she told him. "I want to make sure you can get up the stairs."

"I can. Now, I need razor blades—"

She made a list, using the notepad from her handbag.

"There's a Yankees game tonight," Marcelo said when they had finished.

"Oh, I don't feel like watching them," her father grumbled. "They don't know how to play."

"I hope you realize," Sara said, "that you can't drive over to Woodlawn tomorrow."

"You can drive me."

"I can't. I'll be in school."

"When do you get out of school?"

"Around two-thirty."

"That's too late."

"I could drive you there at seven-thirty."

"That's too early. Monahan's doesn't open until ten."

"Well, I can't arrange my work hours around your hours at Monahan's."

"You're useless," he growled.

"You could walk to St. Brigid," she suggested. "They have a senior citizen's group."

"I'm not going to waste my time with a lot of old bags."

"Then take a taxi over to Woodlawn."

"They don't have taxis in Yonkers."

"Yes, they do. They drive cars like yours."

"I've never seen one."

"You've never looked for one."

Her father considered. "So get a taxi for me. Tell them to pick me up here at eleven tomorrow morning and take me over to Woodlawn."

"Do you want one every day?"

"Every day except Sunday."

"When do you want them to bring you home?"

"Eleven would be fine."

"Eleven to eleven? That's a long day."

"It's a longer day," her father told her, "when I'm alone in this damn house."

"All right. I'll set up a schedule for you."

"They should give me a special rate."

"They should. It's steady business for them."

"It is until I get out of this cast."

"We'll see," she said, remembering what Father Paul had said about miracles. She now had another big one to pray for.

SEVEN

SHE SAT IN a chair in front of the desk waiting for Dr. Vesely to return. The doctor had examined her and taken the usual samples. Three months had passed since her surgery, and nothing had happened other than that one spike in her temperature. Of course there had been only three opportunities for her to conceive during that time, so it could still happen. But with every failure it became harder to revive her hope.

"I'm sorry to keep you waiting," Dr. Vesely said, returning to her office.

"That's okay," Sara said, not minding.

"I can understand why patients might think that all we do is keep them waiting. At times I feel like they could be right."

"I know you do a lot. And I appreciate the time you spend with me."

"Thank you," Dr. Vesely said, gently laying a hand on Sara's shoulder before she sat down. "I wish I could do more for you."

"We didn't solve the problem?"

"It looks like we didn't. From what I can see, an egg was successfully fertilized, but it didn't survive because it was in an inhospitable environment."

"At least it was fertilized."

"Yes. That's progress. But if the egg doesn't survive, then you won't have a baby."

"Are there other things we could try?"

"There are. But they're over the line, and we already went over the line by using syringes."

"I know we did." She didn't teach the doctrine to her third graders, so she didn't know it really well, but she knew enough to understand that using syringes went over the line because it separated procreation from conjugal union. According to the doctrine, it was just as wrong to produce a baby without having sex as it was to have sex without the intent of producing a baby. "But we didn't go far over the line."

"If we tried in vitro, we'd be going farther."

"I guess we would. As I understand it, you'd fertilize a number of eggs and select a few to implant in me. So you'd leave some of the embryos to die."

"In addition," Dr. Vesely said, "by implanting embryos in you, we'd send them to almost certain death."

"You mean because the odds of an embryo surviving in me are almost zero."

"Unfortunately, yes."

"So if we used in vitro and implanted the embryos in me, we'd be killing them."

"We would be."

"Then I don't want to try that."

"I don't either. But I thought you should know your options."

"What else could we try?"

"Well, we could fertilize an egg and implant it in a hospitable environment."

"You mean in another woman's uterus?"

"Yes. And of course that would be over the line."

"I never thought about it, but I'm sure it would be. It also raises other moral issues."

"It does," Dr. Vesely agreed, "beginning with the issue of using a woman for that purpose."

"Why would a woman be willing to do it?"

"To make some money. Or to help a woman who has a problem."

"Wouldn't she want to keep the baby?"

"She might, but you'd have a contract with her."

"So it would be a business deal."

"Yes. It would be."

"Have you ever done one?"

"I wouldn't do it. I've come close to recommending a doctor who would, but something always happens at the last moment."

"You mean a miracle?"

"I mean a change of heart. But that's a kind of miracle."

On her way home she stopped at St. Brigid and found Father Paul, who was in the office that he shared with a woman who did everything that the priests couldn't do.

"Can I talk with you, father?" she asked him.

"Sure," he said, rising from his desk. "I'm due for a booster of nicotine."

The woman shook her head indulgently.

Outside, he lit a cigarette and asked: "How's your father?"

"Oh, he's fine," Sara said. "He's taking a taxi every day to Woodlawn and back."

"He can't leave the old neighborhood."

"No. He can't. And he never will."

Father Paul inhaled and tilted back his head, looking at somewhere beyond the trees. "Your father reminds me of my dad, God rest his soul."

"Do you miss your family?"

"I miss my mum. And I miss my brothers and sisters. But I have a family here."

"You mean your parishioners."

He nodded. "Now, what about you?"

"Well, you know I've been trying to have a baby," she began.

"I didn't know. But I should have guessed."

"I've tried everything. I've even gone over the line. I mean, I haven't gone far, but—"

"I assume you're referring to the doctrine of *Humanae Vitae*."

"My doctor believes that the odds of an embryo surviving in me are almost zero, so I don't want to try in vitro."

"There are other problems with in vitro."

"I know. But an embryo from me could survive if we implanted it in another woman."

"Do you know what the doctrine says about using surrogate mothers?"

"It says that using surrogates is wrong because it separates procreation from conjugal union."

"That's basically it."

"But what if our intentions are good?"

"Your good intentions wouldn't make it right. You know what they say about the road to hell being paved with good intentions."

"My husband and I would be good parents."

"I know you would be. But that doesn't give you a right to have children."

"Well, when I see how other parents raise their children, I feel we do have such a right."

"No one has a right to have children," Father Paul told her. "A child is a gift from God."

"I know, father. But wouldn't it be a gift from God if I get it from another woman?"

"If you pay a woman to carry your child, you reduce it to a commodity. You can't buy a gift from God."

"Then how can I have a baby? I've prayed, and I've prayed, and God just doesn't listen to me."

"He listens to you."

"Then why doesn't He give me a baby?"

"He has His reasons. You have to trust Him."

"I do trust Him. I keep hoping for a miracle, and I even heard Him in a dream telling my husband I would have a baby."

"You mean like your namesake," Father Paul said.

"Is God promising me a baby? Or is He mocking me?"

"I don't think He's doing either. I think He's hoping you'll do the right thing."

"So I shouldn't consider implanting my embryo in another woman."

"From what I can see," Father Paul said, "you have a good marriage. You love your husband, and your husband loves you. If you imitate God's love for you in your love for each other, then you'll be blessed, but in a way that God decides. In other words, don't mess around with test tubes or surrogate mothers."

That evening while they were having dinner she told Marcelo about her conversation with Dr. Vesely.

As always, he listened attentively.

"I agree with your position on trying in vitro," he said when she had finished. "If the odds of an embryo surviving in you are almost zero, what's the point?"

"To show we're trying."

"We know we're trying. Who do we need to show we are?"

"My father," she said, though he wasn't the problem.

"It's not your father you need to show. You've told him what you've done to have a baby, and all he says is, you only have to do what normal couples do."

"You're right. It's my mother. I feel I have to show her I'm trying everything."

"I know you do. But why do you feel that way?"

"I don't know. I guess because I didn't do what she wanted me to do."

"You mean you didn't get married right out of college and have children."

"That's what she wanted," Sara said, appreciating how well he understood the situation.

"But with your condition you couldn't have had children."

"She didn't know about my condition."

"She knows about it now."

"I guess she does."

"And what would she think of sending embryos to an almost certain death?"

"She wouldn't approve of it."

"If neither our church nor your mother would approve of it, then why are you considering it?"

"I'm not considering it, though if an embryo had better odds of surviving in me, I would consider it."

"That wouldn't change the morality of it. But if you decided to try it, I'd support it."

"You'd commit a mortal sin with me?"

"It wouldn't be the first time."

"Well, the odds of an embryo surviving in me are almost zero, so I'm not going to try it. But I could have an embryo implanted in a woman who didn't have a problem."

"You could. But that would raise another moral issue."

"I know it would. But if a woman agreed to have my embryo implanted in her, and if she knew what she was getting into—"

"How would she know?"

"She'd know if she had a baby before."

"She'd only know if she had it under the same conditions."

"And the conditions would never be the same?"

"They never would be."

Sara faced the unavoidable conclusion. "Then she couldn't know what she was getting into."

"She couldn't. So we'd be exploiting her."

"I'm not willing to exploit another person so we can have our own baby."

"I'm not either," Marcelo said.

"We don't have any more options," Sara said after a silence. "I mean, to have our own baby."

"We don't need to have our own baby."

"I wanted to have *your* baby."

"And I wanted to have *your* baby."

"I guess it wasn't in God's plan."

"I guess it wasn't."

"Well, we can keep doing what normal couples do," Sara said, smiling, "but at the same time I think we should start the process of adoption. Do you agree?"

"I agree. And there are so many babies in the world who need parents to raise them, we shouldn't have a problem adopting."

"Maybe we could get a baby from Latin America."

"That would be a good place to find one."

"I assume they're still having babies."

"They are, especially in the Dominican Republic, though they don't like to give their babies up for adoption."

"They would under the right circumstances, wouldn't they?"

"Yeah. So we'll have to look for the right circumstances."

She agreed to see Marcelo the next evening but only for drinks. They met in the bar where they had met the first time, and they went to a booth where they could have privacy.

"You look unhappy," Marcelo said with sympathy after the waiter had brought their drinks.

"I am unhappy."

"I'm sorry."

"I know you are."

"I wish we could start over."

"We can't start over. We're already here."

"And where are we?"

"I don't know. I don't trust you, and without trust—"

"I was honest with you."

"You weren't honest with me upfront."

"All right. I wasn't," he admitted. "But if I'd told you upfront that I was married, we wouldn't be sitting here right now."

"I know, and I wish we weren't." She was sorry the moment she said it. She could see how much it had hurt him. "I'm sorry. I didn't mean that."

"I know you didn't. But I don't blame you."

Her tears started flowing. She couldn't help it. She was crying for the happiness they might have had, for the life they might have had together, for the children they might have had, and for everything they might have had if only he hadn't been married.

He reached out and touched her hand. At that point she saw through the blur of her tears that he was crying too, and she knew it was for the same reason.

"I think we should stop seeing each other for a while," she said with great difficulty.

"Is that what you want to do?"

"It's not what I want to do, it's what I should do."

"Well, I'll do whatever you feel you should do," Marcelo said. "But I have to understand something. You said you didn't trust me. Is that true?"

"I don't know if I should believe you."

"Why shouldn't you?"

"My sister says I shouldn't."

"What does she say you shouldn't believe?"

"She says I shouldn't believe anything you told me, even that you're married."

"Why would I have told you I'm married if I wasn't?"

"So you'd have an excuse not to marry me."

"It's not an excuse not to marry you. It's an obstacle, which I'm going to overcome."

"But if you're not married," Sara said, "then you don't need to get an annulment."

"I *am* married," Marcelo said. "I can show you the documents."

"I don't want to see them."

"I can also show you the papers I filed with the archdiocese."

She shook her head. "I don't want to see them."

"You don't want to see the evidence?"

"If I have to see evidence, we can never have a relationship. I should be able to believe you without evidence."

"You mean you should have faith in me."

"Yes. And I'm having doubts."

"How can I help you overcome your doubts?"

"You can't help me do that. I have to do that by myself."

"You think it'll happen while we're not seeing each other?"

"I think it *won't* happen while we're seeing each other. So give me some time to overcome my doubts."

"How much time do you think you'll need?"

"Well, I might need as much time as you'll need to get an annulment."

He smiled. "That's fair."

They agreed not to see each other for a while, and Marcelo was good about keeping his end of it. He even stopped going to the exercise class so they wouldn't run into each other there.

But he was in her mind, and she couldn't get him out of it. Even at work she lost her focus and thought about him. In her head she presented his case, and then she let Becky argue against him. She knew it was absurd to let her sister influence her since Becky had no experience with men, but at some level she realized that her sister was merely a spokesperson for her mother, and she preferred—even in her head—to deal with her sister.

On the Sunday after she and Marcelo had stopped seeing each other, Sara and Becky took the subway to Woodlawn and went to church with their parents and back to their house for the usual dinner of meat and potatoes.

During dinner their father asked them about their jobs and their mother asked them about their social lives. The opening salvo came from their mother.

"Are you dating anyone?" she asked Sara.

"I'm not dating anyone now," Sara replied, giving her sister a look of warning.

"Well, you're going to be twenty-eight next month, and you're not even close to finding a husband."

"I'm closer than you think," she would have liked to say, but it wasn't true. It was only a hope, a wish, or a dream. Instead, she only said: "I know."

"If you wait too long, then no one will want to marry you."

"Then maybe I'll become a nun," Sara said to bust her mother's chops.

"You don't have a vocation."

"How do you know?"

"If you did, you'd have shown it before."

"Well, I'm a late developer."

"You were a late developer," her father said, referring to her physical development. He hadn't been fooled by the padded bras she had worn in high school.

"When was the last time we had a nun in the family?" Sara asked, pursuing the matter.

"My aunt was a nun," her father said. "She was a Sister of Mercy. She went to Australia."

"Did she like it there?" Sara asked, happy to have changed the subject.

"She loved it there. She stayed there until her death."

"Then what happened? Did they bring her body back to Ireland?"

"No. They left it there. It was her wish to remain there."

"That was your father's sister, right?"

"Right. His older sister."

"I wonder what would have happened if your father had gone to Australia."

"He wouldn't have met my mother, so I would never have been born."

"Then Becky and I would never have been born."

"We shouldn't go too far with that kind of speculation," her mother said. "We should all be happy with the way things are and not wonder how they might have been."

"Then you should be happy with Becky and me the way things are," Sara reasoned.

"I *am* happy with Becky and you. But I'll be happier with both of you when you get married."

"What's wrong with having single daughters?"

"There's nothing wrong with it, up to a point. But with you, Sara, we're reaching that point."

"Well, if you focus more on Becky, maybe she'll get married first." Having just heard a homily about loving people who were difficult to love, Sara refrained from adding that her sister always wanted to be first.

"Maybe I will," Becky said as if she hadn't thought about this possibility of shining in their mother's eyes.

"Are you dating anyone?" her mother asked Becky.

Sara reached for her glass of wine, pleased that on this particular issue she had shifted her mother's attention from her to her sister.

Now that they had made a decision, they began to explore the possibilities of adopting a baby. They were assured by the first counselor they saw that as long as they didn't insist on getting a white baby, they wouldn't have any problem. It would just take time to go through the process.

After talking about it further, she and Marcelo agreed that they had a preference for a baby from Latin America, whatever country. That prompted Sara to contact Clara in Bogotá, who eagerly began working on the project from that end.

Of course they still tried to have a baby doing what normal couples do, and Sara still prayed for a miracle, but she was open to a number of possibilities.

A few weeks after making the decision to adopt a baby she came home from school and found a message from her sister. The message only said to call Becky, which Sara did, and as usual she encountered the secretary, yet another new one.

"Ms. Quinlan's in a meeting," the girl said.

"I'm her sister. She left a message for me to call her."

"Oh. I'll see if I can get her out of the meeting."

Sara waited, and finally the secretary returned and said: "She'll be right with you."

"Are you at home?" Becky asked when she got on the line.

"Yes. I just got home from school."

"Well, I wondered if we could get together."

"Sure," Sara said, immediately sensing that something was wrong. "When?"

"Tonight. I could leave work early and meet you somewhere, so you wouldn't be out late."

"Just tell me where."

"I don't want to make you come into the city. Is there a place in Yonkers where we can meet?"

"There's a bar on Palisade Avenue."

"Does daddy go there?"

"He went there once. He doesn't like it. He says it's full of people who knew mom."

"Then I don't want to go there."

"All right. We could go to a bar in Hastings. I'll pick you up at the Hastings station."

"Do you know when the next train to Hastings is?"

She found the schedule that was stuck to the refrigerator with a magnet. "The next train is at three-twenty."

"I can make that. I'll see you at the Hastings station."

When she spotted Becky among the commuters getting off the train in Hastings, she could tell even from a distance that something had happened to her sister. Of course, her first thought was that Becky had lost her job since that was the most important thing in her life. And she began to prepare some words of comfort and advice.

As her sister approached her, Sara noticed the corporate attire—the gray suit, with the classic white blouse—and she didn't miss having to dress that way. She also noticed that Becky's hair was blond now, with artful highlights.

She hugged her sister and offered to carry the briefcase for her, but Becky thanked her and asked her where they were going.

"To a local bar," Sara told her, "where no one knows us."

"That sounds fine," Becky said docilely.

The bar, which had once been a hangout for employees from Anaconda, was still favored by men who had worked at the plant before it closed. The men at the bar were mostly old since the younger men were still at work, and there were no women.

Sara, who had learned to feel at home in any bar, took her sister's arm and led her to a booth.

Still standing, she asked: "What would you like?"

"A white wine. Any kind."

She went to the bar and got two glasses of white wine.

When she sat down in the booth she looked at Becky, and seeing how utterly miserable she was, she took her sister's hand and said: "Tell me what happened."

"You'll never believe it," Becky said, beginning to cry.

"I will. Tell me."

"I'm pregnant."

"What?" She wasn't at all prepared for this.

"I knew you'd never believe it."

"I do believe it," Sara said, gathering herself. "Why shouldn't I believe it?"

"It shouldn't have happened. It was an accident."

"But why aren't you happy?"

"I didn't want to have a baby," Becky moaned, "and now I don't know what to do."

"Well, I hope you're not thinking of having an abortion."

"No. I'm not. But I don't want to have a baby."

"You should. It's a gift from God."

"Don't give me that bullshit. It's not what I need."

"Then what do you need?"

"I need a solution."

"There is no solution. If you're pregnant, you're going to have a baby. And there's nothing you can do about it. I mean, without committing a sin."

"Marcelo's a doctor," Becky said. "Maybe he knows how I could induce a miscarriage."

"If you did that deliberately, it would be the same as having an abortion."

"It wouldn't be. It would be an accident."

"Well, Marcelo won't tell you how to induce a miscarriage. He's a Catholic like us."

"Then maybe I can find a doctor who will."

"We've been talking about you, but what about Bart?"

"He doesn't know I'm pregnant."

"I assume you're going to tell him."

"No. I'm not," Becky said, shaking her head.

"But as the father, he has a right to know you're pregnant."

"Bart's not the father."

"He's not? Who is?"

"A guy I had sex with in London. I'd drunk too much, and I didn't know what I was doing. I only did it that one time."

"From having that test you knew you were fertile," Sara didn't say. Instead, she said: "Well, it can happen."

"It did happen," Becky said. "And you have to help me find a solution."

EIGHT

WHEN SHE MET Regina for lunch on Saturday she had a lot of news for her friend, but Regina also had news for her which came out as soon as they had been served drinks.

"Guess what," Regina told her. "Joe agreed to buy a house."

"That's great," Sara said, happy for her friend. "Where are you thinking of living?"

"As far away from Joe's mother as possible. But actually, we're going to look for a house in your neighborhood."

"It's a good neighborhood."

"We talked about moving out of Yonkers because the public schools are so dreadful, but we wouldn't send our kids to public schools anyway, so why not live in Yonkers where we can buy a bigger house for the same amount of money?"

"You'll be able to find a house you like in our neighborhood. Do you have an agent?"

"We have one," Regina said, "but I don't like him. He's too much of a salesman."

"I can recommend the agent we used. She understood right away what we were looking for, and she found us a house within a week. It was perfect for us."

"Well, I know what I want, so tell me how to contact her."

"I have her card at home. I'll call you later and give you her phone number."

"That would be great. How's your father?"

"He broke his leg." She told Regina how he had done it. "But that doesn't stop him. He takes a taxi every day to Woodlawn and back."

"That must cost a lot of money."

"I got a special rate for him, but it's still a lot. He's planning to drive there after he gets his cast off. But I don't know."

"What's the problem?"

"His knee is shot. The doctors say he needs a replacement, but he won't even think about it."

"The doctors are full of shit, right?"

"You know my father. But if he can't drive, he can't keep taking a taxi to Woodlawn."

"Maybe he should sell his house and move back there."

"I hadn't thought of that. And he hasn't mentioned it. But it would be a solution."

"With the money he got from selling his house," Regina said, "he could buy or rent an apartment in Woodlawn, and he could walk to Monahan's."

"He could live above Monahan's."

They both laughed.

"Joe and I agreed that if he got out of his old neighborhood, we wouldn't go back to my old neighborhood, so we ruled out Woodlawn."

"I never considered living in Woodlawn. It was a good place to grow up, but I wouldn't want to live there now."

"You still go to church there."

"My father won't go anywhere but St. Barnabas."

"After we move we won't keep going to St. Ann. I don't want to get dragged back into Joe's family, even on Sundays."

"You could go to St. Brigid. They have a nice young Irish priest there."

"Is he cute?" Regina asked wickedly.

"I guess he is. And he really cares about his parishioners. He even cares about my father, though he's not a parishioner."

"Why does everyone care about your father?"

"I don't know. If I weren't his daughter, I probably wouldn't care about him."

"If you weren't his daughter you wouldn't know him, so you probably *would* care about him."

At that moment the waiter came to take their orders.

"So what's happening with you?" Regina asked after lighting a cigarette.

"Marcelo and I have decided to adopt."

"You have? That's great."

"We reached the point where we knew we couldn't have our own baby without going way over the line, and we didn't want to do that."

"I assume you're talking about in vitro."

"That or using a surrogate mother."

"I read about in vitro. The odds aren't very good, and there's a risk of birth defects."

"There's a risk of birth defects however you have a baby."

"Yeah, but they're higher with in vitro. And even if the church weren't against it, I don't like the idea of conceiving a baby in a test tube."

"I think they use a petri dish."

"Whatever they use, I don't like the idea. And as for using a surrogate mother, I could never use another woman for that purpose. And it's not because I'm a Catholic."

"I understand. Though it might have been tempting."

"A lot of things are tempting," Regina said. "I don't know how many times I was tempted to kill Joe's mother, but I never once reached for a knife. I never even raised the knife that was already in my hand."

"But how would you feel," Sara asked, "if the church said that it was all right?"

"All right to kill Joe's mother?"

Sara laughed. "All right to use a surrogate."

"I still wouldn't do it. I wouldn't even consider it."

"But there are people who would consider it."

"There are people who do it. And I'm not judging them. I don't have any right to judge people. But for people who are wavering, it's probably helpful for our church to say it's morally wrong. At least it stops some people from doing things they might regret."

"It didn't stop me, but it did support me in my decision."

"So where are you looking for a baby?"

"We're looking everywhere," Sara said. "But we're going to focus on Latin America."

"They have a lot of babies there. I see them in ads for saving the children."

"Those babies are adorable. But then all babies are adorable."

"We're going to give ourselves another year," Regina said. "And if nothing happens, we're going to adopt."

"Well, maybe it will help if you have your own house."

"It'll be less stressful, that's for sure."

While they were eating, Sara released her other big news item. "My sister Becky is pregnant."

"What?" Regina stared at her in disbelief. "I thought she didn't want to have children."

"She doesn't. It was an accident."

"An accident? And we're trying to get pregnant on purpose. It doesn't seem fair."

"For us it would be a blessing. For her it's a problem, and she doesn't know what to do about it."

"She wouldn't have an abortion, would she?"

"No. She's still a Catholic."

"Then she better get used to the idea of being a mother."

"I can't imagine her being a mother."

"I can't either," Regina agreed.

"So she has a problem," Sara said, "and she wants me to help her find a solution."

"That's Becky. She never solved her own problems."

"She always went to mom."

"And now she comes to you. But if she wouldn't have an abortion, and if she doesn't want a baby, then the only solution is to have the baby and put it up for adoption."

"What if she gave the baby to me?"

"You really think she'd do that?"

"She might. I mean, if it was the only solution."

Regina considered. "It would be a solution for you. The baby would have your genes, so it's as close to being your own baby as you could get."

"That's what I was thinking."

"Your sister would be a natural surrogate. And since you didn't have anything to do with her getting pregnant, you wouldn't have a problem with the church."

"It would avoid a lot of problems."

"What about her husband?"

"It's not his baby, so he wouldn't want it."

"Your sister had a love affair?"

"It wasn't an affair, it was a one-night stand."

"I didn't know she had it in her."

"I didn't either. But according to her, that's what happened."

"Well, sooner or later her husband will notice she's pregnant. So what'll she tell him?"

"She'll tell him the truth."

"If she had an abortion, he'd never know."

"Yeah, that would be the easy way, but I can't imagine her having an abortion."

"I can't imagine her having a one-night stand with a guy."

Pursuing the matter, Sara asked: "So what do you think about the idea of her giving me the baby?"

"It sounds like the perfect solution. And I have no doubt that you'd make a far better mother than Becky. But I don't think it would ever work."

"Why wouldn't it?"

"You really think a woman could give her baby to her sister unless she was dying or incapacitated?"

"I think a woman could."

"Maybe you could, but not Becky. So don't get your hopes up."

"Don't worry. I've learned not to get my hopes up."

That evening before dinner she told Marcelo about her idea. It was warm enough to sit outside, so they were on the porch drinking wine and enjoying the view of the river.

"I can see your sister putting the baby up for adoption," he said after reflecting, "but I can't see her giving it to you."

"Why not?"

"Because if she gave it to you, then you'd have something she didn't have."

"I already have things she doesn't have."

"But you don't have a baby."

"Well, if she knows I want it, then maybe she'll want it."

"If she wants it, then she'll keep it."

"But if she keeps it only because I want it, would that be good for the baby?"

"I don't know. If you both had children, she'd try to be a better mother than you."

She gazed at the river, remembering how her sister had always tried to outshine her but recognizing that in this situation it wouldn't be a bad thing. "If it made her keep it, then what harm could come from my offering to take the baby?"

"She might not want it enough to keep it," Marcelo said, "but she might not want you to have it, so she might get rid of it."

"You mean put it up for adoption?"

"I mean have an abortion."

"She wouldn't do that. She'd only do that if she didn't have any other solution. And by offering to take the baby, I'd give her a solution."

"So you think it would stop her from having an abortion?"

"She wouldn't even think about having an abortion."

"How do you know?"

"She's my sister. We were raised the same way. She wouldn't think about having an abortion any more than she'd think about getting a divorce."

"Then you don't need to offer to take the baby to stop her from having an abortion."

"That's not why I would do it."

"I think I heard you using that as a justification."

"I didn't mean it that way. I meant that if she didn't have any other solution, it would give her a solution. But I don't have to justify offering to take a baby she doesn't want."

"Of course you don't have to, but you feel you do."

"It's not enough that I want the baby?"

"It should be enough. But I think you're trying to do two things at the same time."

"You mean I'm trying to do something for my sister, and I'm also trying to do something for myself?"

"That's what it sounds like."

"So I shouldn't try to solve her problem?"

"I'm not saying you shouldn't, I'm only saying it shouldn't be your primary motive."

"Okay. You're right. I shouldn't think about Becky or myself. I should think about the baby."

"I think you're on the right track now."

"Well, don't you think we'd make better parents?"

"I know we would," Marcelo said. "But that doesn't give us the right to take a baby away from your sister."

"I wouldn't take it away from her. I'd offer to take it off her hands. And if she agreed, she'd give it to me."

Marcelo considered. "She might agree to give it to you, but she might not let you keep it."

"If she didn't want it, why wouldn't she let me keep it?"

"Because it would be *her* baby."

"I wouldn't mind sharing it with her."

"Then it would have two mothers."

"At some point we'd have to tell it that my sister was its birth mother. But that happens in most adoptions."

"It does. And if you had a better relationship with your sister, it might not be a major problem."

"If we shared a baby, it might improve our relationship."

"It might. But it might not."

"And if it didn't, then we could have problems." She watched an empty tanker gliding down river, riding the current and the outgoing tide. "So you think it's a bad idea."

"I didn't say that. I just said that you have to be clear about why you want to do it."

She looked deep inside herself and found the reason. "I want to do it because I believe it would be better for the baby."

"So you want to do it for the same reason that you would adopt any baby, no matter who the mother was?"

"Yes. I do," she said with certainty.

"Then tell your sister you have a solution," Marcelo said supportively. "And see what she thinks of it."

As the days passed she should have gotten used to not seeing him. Being apart from him should have gotten easier. But it didn't get easier, it got harder.

During the day she immersed herself in work, but even then she couldn't get him out of her mind, and there were limits to how long she could work. By nine o'clock even the people in California had gone home, so there was no one for her to talk to.

After leaving work she headed for the nearest bar. She avoided going to the bars in her neighborhood for fear of running into a former boyfriend who would remind her of how silly, how shallow, and how immature she had been. She hadn't had the faintest idea of what love was, and now that she knew what it was, she had no respect for her former self. But what good was the respect she had earned for her present self by not going out with a married man? It had only made her miserable.

She also avoided going to her apartment, where she would run into her sister. She had learned from that one experience not to share her feelings with Becky, and she couldn't help blaming Becky for her situation. If she hadn't told her sister about Marcelo and revealed the fact that he was married, she might have kept seeing him. But through her sister she had heard her mother's voice, and she couldn't ignore it. Whatever justifications you might have, the voice told her in no uncertain terms, you shouldn't go out with married men.

Luckily, she and her sister had their own bedrooms, so Becky couldn't hear her crying at night, soaking her pillow on one side, then turning it over and soaking it on the other side. The tears kept coming as if she would never run out of them. Time was supposed to heal everything, but the wound didn't close, and the pain didn't begin to go away.

One Saturday afternoon, as she was walking down Second Avenue after leaving her favorite pumps at the shoe repair shop to get the worn-out heels replaced, she almost literally ran into Marcelo, who was walking toward her.

Ironically, he was so much on her mind that she didn't see him coming, and by the time she did there was no way of getting around him.

"Hi," he said, stopping in front of her.

"Hi," she said, her heart pounding.

"How are you?"

"I'm fine. How are you?"

"You want to know the truth?"

She did, and she didn't, so she didn't know what to say.

"The truth is," Marcelo told her with glistening eyes, *"estoy muriendo sin ti."*

"That's how I feel. I'm dying without you."

"Could we go somewhere and talk?"

"Sure." She spotted a bar where she had gone in the distant past, and she pointed toward it. "We could go there."

They went into the bar and found an empty booth in back.

She was thankful that the light in the bar was so dim because the last time she had looked in a mirror she had seen a face ravaged by pain.

The waiter came to take their orders.

"I'll have a white wine," she said.

"I'll have a Corona," he said.

They sat in an awkward silence, waiting for their drinks.

When the waiter had left them, Marcelo said: "I have some good news."

"You do? I could use some."

"The woman I married has finally agreed to testify in the hearing." She must have looked blank because he explained:

"The hearing in my annulment process. She wasn't cooperating before, but now she is. She must have found another guy she wants to marry."

"That's good," she said, beginning to feel a little better.

"It'll speed up the process. So instead of taking another year, it could take only another month. And I can make sure it doesn't take any longer by giving a donation."

"Is that how famous people get annulments?"

"Oh, yeah. I didn't consider giving a donation. I didn't have any reason to. But now I do."

She was touched by his willingness to sacrifice the purity of the process for her sake.

"Since it's going to happen," Marcelo said, looking her directly in the eye, "I'm in a position to ask you to marry me."

With tears forming she returned his look.

"I've tried not seeing you, and it proved something beyond any doubt. It proved I can't live without you."

"It proved the same thing to me."

"So will you marry me?"

Without hesitation she said: "I will."

"Thank God," he said, reaching for her hand.

"I want to have your children," she said, letting the tears flow down her cheeks. She didn't have to say: "And I don't care what color they are."

"I want you to have your children."

"I love you," she said.

"I love you too."

Now that they were formally engaged, she started spending weekends at his apartment. She warned her sister that if she tattled on her or gave their mother any reason to suspect what she was doing, she would make up something worse about Becky and tell it to their mother.

So Becky cooperated. If their mother called while she was at Marcelo's apartment, Becky would say she was out on an errand, and then she would call Sara and let her know that their mother had called, and Sara would call her mother from Marcelo's apartment, pretending to be at her own apartment. As far as she knew, her mother never guessed what was going on. But her mother did guess she had a boyfriend.

"Are you serious about him?" her mother asked while they were talking on the phone.

"I am," she said with a glance at Marcelo, who was lying next to her in bed. "I'm very serious about him."

"So when are we going to meet him?"

"Soon. I just have to find a weekend when he's not working."

"He works on weekends? What does he do?"

"He's a doctor. He works in the emergency room at New York Hospital. But he does get some weekends off."

"Then why don't you bring him here on a Sunday?"

"When he has a Sunday off, he usually sees his mother."

"Where does she live?"

"In the Bronx."

"The Bronx?"

"Don't say it that way. We're from the Bronx."

"You are, but I'm not. I'm from Yonkers."

"What's the difference?"

"The Bronx is the Bronx, and Yonkers is Yonkers."

"Oh. I see," she said, smiling. She reached out and stroked the back of Marcelo's head.

"Is he Irish?"

"No. He's Dominican."

"He's Hispanic?"

"Yeah. He was born in Santo Domingo, but his parents moved here when he was little."

"What does he look like?"

"He's very handsome."

"I meant—" Her mother abruptly stopped. "Oh, forget it. Bring him home so we can meet him."

"I'll ask him what would be a good Sunday."

"Now, would you put Becky on the line? I want to ask her something."

Of course her sister was at their apartment, where Sara was pretending to be. "She went out to do an errand. I'll have her call you when she gets back."

"All right. Well, let me know what Sunday you're coming."

"Whew," she said after hanging up. She did a pantomime of wiping sweat off her brow.

"So she wants to meet me."

"She does, and she'll love you."

"How do you know?"

"You're the kind of man she dreamed I'd marry."

"She dreamed you'd marry a brown man?"

"You're a nice person. You're a doctor. My mother won't care what color you are."

"What about your father?"

"He'll care. But his racism is only skin deep. When he gets to know you, he'll love you."

"You think he will?"

"If you talk with him about baseball, you'll bond together."

"I assume your father's a Yankees fan."

"He's from the Bronx."

"Then we have some essential things in common. We're from the same borough, and we're for the same team."

"But you don't drive the same kind of car."

"What kind of car does he drive?"

"A Crown Victoria."

"That's a cop car."

"It's also a taxi."

"So he wouldn't drive a Japanese car?"

"My father was a marine," she explained. "He fought in the battle of Guadalcanal. He shot a Japanese soldier out of a tree and stopped him from killing one of his buddies. He has a piece of shrapnel in his leg from a Japanese mortar."

"Then we should take the subway there."

"It's the easiest way."

On Monday after school she took her father to St. John's to have his cast removed. The orthopedist had doubts that he would be able to walk without a knee replacement, but to prove the doctor wrong her father started walking without crutches.

It was like at Lourdes when a lame pilgrim threw away his crutches and started walking.

"You see?" her father said. "I can walk perfectly."

"But aren't you in pain?" the doctor asked.

"You don't even know what pain is, so why are you asking?"

"I'm asking because I'm concerned about you."

"You're not concerned about me. You just want to make some easy money."

"It's not easy to do a knee replacement."

"It's easier than working for a living."

The doctor shrugged. "Whatever you say."

As they were leaving the hospital her father took her arm.

"Are you okay?" she asked him.

"Yeah. I'm okay. I just have to get used to not having a cast on my leg."

"It gave you support. You should have kept the crutches. Should I go back and get them?"

"No. I don't need them. But maybe I could use a cane."

"You're going to have physical therapy tomorrow. You can ask them for a cane then."

"What do I need therapy for?"

"To help you walk."

"It won't help me walk, and it'll cost money."

"The therapy will help you. And it won't cost you anything."

"Someone has to pay for it."

"Medicare will pay for it. But you contributed to Medicare, so you're entitled to get something back."

"If all those colored people get it, then I should get it. At least I worked. They didn't do anything but go on welfare."

With difficulty she refrained from pursuing that subject.

After taking her father to his house she stopped at Barca Brothers, the local supermarket on Palisade, and then went to her house, where she called her sister. She had let the idea of offering to take the unwanted baby gestate in her mind, and now she felt it was time for delivery.

"I have a solution," she told her sister.

"You do? What is it?" Becky sounded hopeful.

"I can't tell you over the phone, but I don't want to leave you in suspense, so take a train to Hastings and I'll meet you at the station. We can go to that bar and talk there."

"Is there a four-twenty train?"

"Yes." She knew without checking.

"Then I'll be on that."

This time her sister got off the train and went along with her without asking any questions. The only difference was that now Becky ordered a club soda instead of a white wine, which Sara found encouraging. At least it indicated that Becky cared about the health of her baby.

When they had settled in a booth Sara said: "Before I tell you my solution, I need to know if you want this baby."

"I don't want it," Becky said, shaking her head emphatically. "A baby is the last thing I want. It would wreck my career."

"So what are you planning to do with it?"

"I don't know. I'll probably have it and put it up for adoption. I just have to tell Bart what happened."

"He doesn't know yet?"

"He hasn't noticed anything."

"Then maybe you can slip the baby by him."

Becky frowned. "Do you always have to laugh about things?"

"It's better than always crying about them."

"You never cried."

"I cried," she said, remembering how she had cried over being separated from Marcelo.

"But you never had this kind of thing happen to you."

"I've been praying for this kind of thing to happen to me."

"Then you should have a baby."

"My doctor says I can't have one."

Becky deliberated, and then she quietly asked: "Would you like to have my baby?"

"You mean you'd give it to me?"

"Yes. I don't want it, and if you want it you can have it."

She hadn't dared to imagine it would be so easy. "That was the solution I was going to propose."

"It was? Well, I'm glad I offered it before you asked me. But the thing is," Becky continued, making a face of extreme torment, "I still have to tell Bart about it."

"If you tell him the baby isn't his, he won't want it."

"He won't want it. But he might want me to have an abortion."

"I hope he couldn't make you do it."

"He can't make me do anything. But I don't want this baby to wreck my marriage."

Sara couldn't see what there was to wreck, but she respected her sister's commitment to the institution. "Well, he shouldn't expect you to lose your soul to save your marriage."

"No. He shouldn't. But he might expect me to get rid of the evidence that I was unfaithful to him."

"My husband wouldn't expect me to do that."

"You mean your husband would accept the fact that you got pregnant from another man?"

"I wouldn't put him in that position."

"But what if you did?"

"I know he wouldn't want me to have an abortion."

"Would he want you to keep the baby?"

"I think he would. I mean, he knows how much I want one."

"Well, I don't want one," Becky said. "And I can't imagine Bart wanting me to keep it."

"Then we have a solution."

"I think we do."

They shook on it as they used to shake on pacts they made on the rare occasions when they were getting along as sisters.

NINE

WALKING TO HER father's house after school the next day, she saw Father Paul in front of the church, and it occurred to her that his smoking habit gave him a reason for standing where he could talk with people walking by.

"Hi, father," she said brightly.

"Hi, Sara. How are you?"

"I'm fine, thanks. How are you?"

"I'm enjoying this moment."

"You mean smoking or talking with me?"

"Both," he said, smiling. "How's your father?"

"He's recovering. You should have seen him at the hospital after they took his cast off. He threw away his crutches like a pilgrim at Lourdes."

"And he didn't fall on his bum?"

"No. He walked out on his own steam."

"I saw him walking this morning. It must have been painful, but he didn't show it."

"He never would. But he shows it in other ways," she added.

"I can imagine."

"I'm hoping that with the physical therapy the pain in his knee will go away, and then he won't need a replacement."

"What does the doctor say about that?"

"He says it'll take more than physical therapy."

"And he doesn't mean a miracle."

"No. He means surgery."

"Well, there I'm on your father's side. They should at least try to fix things before they replace them."

"You mean like with cars."

126

"They don't fix anything in cars now," Father Paul said. "They don't know how to. They only know how to take out the old part and put in a new one."

"That's what they do with my car. I wonder what they'd do if they couldn't get new parts."

"They'd learn how to fix things."

"So let's hope the physical therapist knows how to fix my father's knee."

"Let's pray that she does."

"How do you know it's a woman?"

"Your father told me."

"I won't ask what he said about her."

"He said she was a healthy girl. He wouldn't have gone into the titillating details with me."

"I guess he wouldn't have," Sara said. "Do you ever miss hearing male talk?"

"At times," Father Paul said. "And then I go to that bar on Palisade and have a small one."

Sara laughed. "I can picture you there."

"You've been there?"

"Once or twice."

"Do you go there with colleagues after a bad day?"

"I never have a bad day."

"I guess you wouldn't. Then you must take colleagues there to console them."

"I take them there to celebrate."

"Now that you mention it, you look like you have something to celebrate. What is it?"

She had wanted to tell him, so she took the opening. "My husband and I made a decision. We're going to adopt."

"That's wonderful," Father Paul said, smiling.

"You helped me make the decision."

"I did?" He looked as if he had no idea how he might have helped her.

"When you told me not to mess with test tubes or surrogate

mothers, you made me realize that I was on the wrong track, and you put me onto the right track."

"You were already on the right track. You only needed some reassurance."

"I did need reassurance. And I got it from you."

"Will you give me a testimonial?"

"Sure. I'll tell the cardinal."

"Just tell Father Scanlon. That will be enough." He took a drag on his cigarette, and then he said: "I assume that you and your husband are together on this."

"We're absolutely together on it."

"Then somewhere in the world there's a lucky child."

She wanted to tell him she knew exactly where in the world the child was, but she didn't because she felt it would have been tempting fate.

Looking up the street, she could see her father's car in the driveway, so she concluded that he hadn't yet tried to drive to Woodlawn. She assumed that he had taken a taxi there and wouldn't be home until around five.

She approached his house and opened the outer door, which would have been locked from the inside if he had been there, and she let herself in. She was met by the cat, who stared at her as if he wondered what she was doing there.

She reached down and scratched his neck, aware of the smoke that emanated from his fur.

As usual, the living room was a mess. There were newspapers scattered around the floor and dirty dishes on the tables.

She picked up things in the living room. She ran a load of dishes, she put the milk and orange juice cartons back into the refrigerator, she removed an empty tuna can from the kitchen floor, and she inspected the powder room, which made her gag.

"You should hire a cleaning woman," her mother told her.

"I hired one. She came here once, and he sent her away."

"Then you should clean the house yourself."

"What do you think I'm doing now?"

She was scrubbing the toilet when her father came home, jangling his keys.

"I'm here," she called out, so he would know she was in the house and not have a heart attack upon entering the powder room and bumping into her.

"Sara? Is that you?"

"No, it's an elf."

He appeared in the doorway and watched her scrub the toilet for a while before he finally asked: "What are you doing?"

"I'm cleaning your filthy toilet."

"It hasn't been cleaned in a long time."

"I don't know how you can live in this house."

"I don't know either," her father said. "I'm thinking of selling it and living somewhere else."

She straightened up, still holding the brush that she had been using as a weapon in her attack on the stains. "You are?"

"I never wanted to come here in the first place. It was your mother's idea. And now that she's gone, there's no reason for me to stay here."

From her perspective there *was* a reason for him to stay here: it was within walking distance of her house, so it was easier for her to take care of him. But he didn't need this house. And since she had never lived here, she felt no attachment to it. "Where would you go?"

"Back to Woodlawn. If we hadn't sold our house there, I could be living in it, on the ground floor, so I wouldn't have to go up and down stairs."

"Maybe you could buy it back from the people you sold it to."

"They want too much for it."

"You asked them?"

"Yeah. You think I just sit at Monahan's and do nothing?"

"How much do they want for it?"

"They want three hundred and fifty thousand."

"For that house? They do want too much."

"I told you they did. And I'd be lucky to get two hundred thousand for this house."

"You'd be lucky to get anything the way it looks now."

"I'd have it cleaned professionally, and I'd have it painted. That's all it needs."

"Then this amateur is putting down her brush."

He looked down into the toilet bowl and said: "You didn't do such a bad job."

"Thanks, dad. You really know how to motivate people."

"Would you like a drink?" he asked as she followed the line of the cat and her father into the kitchen.

"What are you offering?"

"Beer or whisky."

"You don't have wine?"

"Why would I have wine?"

"For guests," she suggested.

"I never have guests."

"Then I'll have a beer."

He opened the refrigerator and got out two bottles, which he opened on the counter.

"How's your knee?" she asked, taking a cold bottle from him.

"It's fine," he said as if there was no reason to ask.

"It's not painful when you walk on it?"

"No, not at all."

"You mentioned not having to go up and down stairs. Is that hard for you?"

"It's my favorite activity."

She took a swig of beer. It tasted good after the housework. "If you move back to Woodlawn, you should find an apartment on the ground floor."

"It's hard to find an apartment on the ground floor."

"Then you should live in a building with an elevator."

"I don't like elevators. And even if I did, there aren't many buildings with elevators."

"You mean in Woodlawn."

"I'm not going anywhere else."

"So the only thing that'll work for you is the ground floor of our old house?"

"I could live on the ground floor of another house."

"Would you have to own the house?"

"I always owned the houses I lived in."

"It might be easier not to own it."

"How could it be easier? I'd have to deal with a landlord."

"And the landlord would have to deal with you," she didn't say. "Well, after the school year ends, I could drive you there and help you look for a place to live."

"It would save money on taxis," he said.

She wasn't sure if he meant that her driving him to Woodlawn or his moving there would save money on taxis. He could have meant both.

Her mother had wanted them to come with Becky and go to mass at St. Barnabas, but Sara didn't want to put her father on the spot by arriving with a "colored" man, without any warning, and giving her father no alternative but to walk into church with this man in front of all his friends, who generally shared his racist attitudes. In order to avoid this situation she told her mother that Marcelo always went with his family to an eleven o'clock mass in Spanish, that she would go with him, and that they would take the subway from there.

"You understand the mass in Spanish?" her mother asked.

"I understand most of it."

"What church do they go to?"

"St. Martin of Tours."

"I've never been there."

"It's a nice church," Sara said, though she had never been there either. It was the church that Marcelo's family attended, and it did have masses in Spanish.

When the day came she felt that they should go to church with his family so she wouldn't be lying to her mother, but they didn't get up in time.

As they walked to her house from the subway station she reminded Marcelo to engage her father in a conversation about baseball.

"I'm ready," he said as if he had studied for an exam.

Her mother greeted them at the door, and Sara noticed the look of relief in her mother's eyes upon seeing that Marcelo was lighter than she had expected. Her mother then shifted into the mode of warmly welcoming the man who would rescue Sara from being an old maid, thanks be to God after all those years of maternal anxiety.

They found her father on the back porch, smoking a cigar.

"Dad, this is Marcelo," she said hopefully.

Her father scrutinized Marcelo without moving or taking the cigar out of his mouth.

"I'm very pleased to meet you, sir," Marcelo said, extending his hand.

Her father didn't take the hand. "Marcelo. Are you Italian?"

"I'm Dominican," Marcelo said. "Like your cigar."

"How can you tell my cigar is Dominican?"

"From its aroma. Is it a Cohiba?"

"No. It's a Montecristo."

"You have good taste in cigars, sir."

"I smoke the good ones only on Sundays. I can't afford to smoke them every day." All this time her father had been talking through his teeth, which were clamped on the cigar, but now he finally took the cigar out of his mouth and said: "I understand that you're a doctor."

"Yes. I am."

"What kind of doctor?"

"I'm planning to be a family practitioner."

"Is that like a general practitioner?"

"Yes. They used to call it that."

"So you'll know a little about everything but not much about anything."

"I won't know much," Marcelo admitted, "but I'll know enough to treat people and help them."

"Did you study medicine on some island?"

"Yes. The island of Manhattan."

"He went to Cornell Medical School," Sara told her father.

"Cornell? Isn't that upstate?"

"Cornell University is upstate," Marcelo said, "but the medical school is in Manhattan."

Her father puffed on his cigar. "Your country produces some good baseball players."

"You mean Rafael Belliard, Julio Franco, Tony Fernandez, and Juan Samuel?"

"Don't forget Alfredo Griffin and Rafael Ramírez."

"And Juan Marichal."

"You don't have to pay those guys so much. You know how much they're paying Mattingly?"

"They're paying him one million nine hundred and seventy-five thousand dollars."

Her father was visibly impressed. "He's not worth it. That's the problem with the game now. It's all about money. It's not a sport anymore."

"It's a business," Marcelo agreed.

"And with all the money they pay for those players, they still can't win. They couldn't even beat the Red Sox last season."

"The Red Sox didn't have a bad team."

"Maybe not, but the Red Sox are jinxed. Did you see how they lost that game to the Mets in the World Series?"

"The ball went right between Buckner's legs."

It was going much better than Sara had expected. And she knew exactly what Marcelo could give her father as a birthday present—a box of Montecristos.

The next evening, after an inexplicably tense phone conversation with her mother, she agreed to go and see her parents the next Sunday, without Marcelo or Becky, so that she could explain the situation to them. Her mother's use of the word "situation" didn't bode well.

She timed her arrival so that they would have just returned from church, believing they would be most tolerant and forgiving then. She found her mother in the kitchen preparing dinner, and she was relieved that her father was out on the porch smoking.

Whatever the problem, she expected her mother to be more understanding than her father.

She hugged her mother dutifully and offered to help.

"Thanks," her mother said. "I have everything under control. Would you like some coffee?"

"Sure, if it's already made." She recognized the offer as an invitation to sit down at the kitchen table and have a talk.

Her mother brought two mugs of coffee and sat down opposite her.

She waited, not wanting to make the first move.

"I like Marcelo," her mother said, looking at her directly. "But I don't like the situation."

"What situation?" She wondered if her mother had guessed that she was spending weekends at Marcelo's apartment.

"You know what I'm talking about. He's a married man."

"How did you find out?"

"Becky told me."

"That little rat," she didn't say. "Well, technically he is, but he wasn't ever really married, and he's getting an annulment."

"Annulments take a long time."

"He's been working on it a long time, and he expects to get it. So don't worry."

"But he's still married."

"Yes, he's still married. But as soon as he gets his annulment, he's going to marry me."

"Are you sure?"

"Yes. I trust him completely. I love him, and I want to share my life with him."

Her mother nodded understandingly. "I'm glad you feel that way about him. But as long as he's married, you shouldn't go out with him."

"I tried not seeing him for a while, and I couldn't bear it."

"How long did you try not seeing him?"

"For almost a month."

Her mother sighed. "If you couldn't bear not seeing him for a month, then you're in trouble."

"Don't worry, mom. He'll get an annulment."

"How soon do you think he'll get it?"

"By the end of the summer. He made a donation to speed things up."

"All right. And how soon after that would you get married?"

She began to have the impression that her mother was worried about her getting pregnant and her not being able to get married in time to cover it up. "As soon as possible. But we can't set a date for the wedding until he has the annulment."

"Well, if you wait too long, you won't be able to schedule a wedding in the fall."

"You mean at St. Barnabas."

"Your father will want to have the wedding there," her mother said as if there was no question about it.

On this point Sara was more than willing to accommodate her father. "Does he know about Marcelo?"

"I haven't told him. And I'm not going to tell him."

"Will Becky tell him?"

"No. She'll assume I told him."

"Well, I think he hit it off with dad. What do you think?"

"Your father likes him. But he's not going to like the idea of you marrying him."

"I had a feeling he might not like it. But that's his problem."

"It's your problem too. You have to deal with him."

"Why do I have to deal with him?" Sara asked. "I'm only his daughter. You're his wife."

"You think I don't deal with him every day?"

"I'm sorry. I only meant—"

"I know what you meant. And it's all right. In some ways, you're better at dealing with him than I am. Maybe because you're his gift from God."

"I never thought of myself that way. I always thought I was his pain in the ass."

"No. Becky's his pain in the ass."

"So how am I going to deal with a racist?"

"You're going to convince him that Marcelo is the best son-in-law he could ever have."

"Okay. I'll try." She sipped her coffee. "But he could have the same problem as the woman that Marcelo married."

"What problem did she have?"

"She was afraid of having a black baby."

"Poor Marcelo," her mother said with sympathy. "I'm glad you told me that. I was already on his side, but now I'm on his side all the way."

"Thanks, mom. Now, how do I get dad on his side?"

"You get him to see Marcelo as you see him."

"But how do I overcome the racism?"

"That's only in your father's head. It's not in his heart. He has a good heart."

At that moment the man in question came into the kitchen through the back door, still holding a lighted cigar.

"Jack," her mother said, "you know the rule about cigars in the house."

"I was just checking to see if dinner's almost ready," her father said. "If it's not, I don't want to put this out and then have to light it again. It's a Montecristo."

"It's going to be another twenty minutes, so why don't you go back out and enjoy your cigar. I'll call you when it's ready."

He went back out, fanning the air behind him.

"This would be a good time," her mother advised her, "to start working on him."

"Okay. I guess not much can go wrong in twenty minutes."

"A lot can go wrong in almost no time, so you have to handle him with care."

She went out the back door and found her father sitting in one of the outside chairs that he had repaired so many times.

"Hi, dad," she said, leaning against the wrought-iron railing. "How are you doing?"

"I'm doing fine," her father growled. "I've been sitting here trying to find something wrong with that guy you brought home last Sunday."

"You always did find something wrong with the guys I brought home," she said, smiling.

"There was always something wrong with them."

"You're right. There was."

"Now, there're a lot of things right with this guy. He's smart. He knows cigars. He knows baseball. And he's a doctor, which is a good thing to have in a family."

"But—" she said, providing the word she knew was coming.

"With all the things that are right with him, why couldn't he have been a white guy?"

"You mean why didn't God make him a white guy?"

"You know," her father said, "there are times when I wonder if God really knows what He's doing. Sooner or later I come around to the view that He does. But this time I don't know if I'm going to come around to that view."

"Why should this time be any different?"

"This time it involves you."

"So what are you worried about?"

"You know damned well what I'm worried about."

"You're worried," she said point blank, "about the color of your grandson if I marry Marcelo."

"Well, I can't see myself walking around the neighborhood with a black grandson."

"You walked around the neighborhood with a black Irish daughter."

"I still don't know where we got you," he muttered.

"Mom said I was a gift from God."

"You *were* a gift from God," he said with bare emotion, "and I was so thankful when you arrived."

"I hope you still are."

He spat a piece of tobacco over the railing. "I am. But I wonder why you couldn't have done what your friends did."

"You mean get married right after college, have two kids, and then get divorced?"

"I can think of only two of your friends who got divorced."

"There are more coming, believe me."

"Do you really like this guy?" her father asked after a long thoughtful silence.

"I love him, dad. I know he's the right man for me."

"You're sure?"

"I'm sure."

"Well, he knows cigars, and he knows baseball," her father said as if those were the two main requirements for an acceptable son-in-law.

After leaving her father's house she drove to the Korean grocery store in Dobbs Ferry, where among other fruits and vegetables she bought some mangos and a papaya. Instead of going home via Broadway she went around the block and headed for the parkway, prompted by what she had seen on the news the night before. A doctor at a clinic that did abortions had been shot and killed by a protester. It had happened in Georgia or Alabama, and it made her feel like driving by the women's clinic in Dobbs Ferry to see what was happening there.

As usual there were about a dozen people standing out in front of the clinic with their signs. Among them she spotted the old woman she had given a ride to. But the person who stood out from the group was a tall man with flowing blond hair and a beard who could have been a model for a painting of Jesus. He was wearing a white monk's habit, with a large wooden cross hanging from a chain around his neck. She hadn't noticed him before, and she wondered if his appearance on the scene marked a new phase of the protests.

That evening, as she and Marcelo were sitting on the porch having drinks before dinner, she told him about seeing the monk at the clinic.

"Are you sure he was a real monk?" Marcelo asked.

"He looked real. But he could have been a fake."

"Next time you see this monk," Marcelo joked, "ask for his credentials."

She laughed. "I will. The reason I drove by there is, I was thinking about that doctor who was shot and killed yesterday."

"It always happens with protesters. When they don't get what they want, then some of them resort to violence. It happened with the protesters against the war in Vietnam. Some of them began killing in the name of peace."

She had been in grade school at the time, so it hadn't been an important life event for her. It hadn't even been covered by her college course in American history. But she had seen movies about the war in Vietnam, so she knew what Marcelo was talking about. "And now some of these protesters have begun killing in the name of life."

"They evidently don't see the irony of it."

"To see the irony of something," Sara said, "you have to be detached from it."

"The people who kill doctors at abortion clinics must have a personal reason for doing it. At least I hope they're not doing it for an ideological reason."

"Would that be worse?"

"I think it would be," Marcelo said. "If they're doing it for a personal reason, then they're doing it for revenge. And that's more understandable."

"But is it more justifiable?"

"It's never justifiable to kill someone."

"What if you were back in the emergency room and they brought in a pregnant woman, and the only way you could save her life was to do an abortion?"

"I'd try to save both of them. I wouldn't sacrifice the baby for the mother."

"What if the mother asked you to?"

"I still wouldn't do it."

"Would you sacrifice the mother for the baby?"

"You mean if she asked me to?"

"Yeah. Would you?"

"Well, that's different. At least the mother can tell me what she wants. The baby can't."

"So would you sacrifice her?"

Marcelo shook his head. "I'd try to save both of them."

"What if you couldn't?"

"I'd still try."

"Even if by trying you endangered both of them?"

"Man, you ask tough questions."

"I guess they're tougher than the questions a woman has to answer when she considers having an abortion. But it still must be tough for a woman in that situation."

"Having a choice is always tough."

Two weeks later the school year ended, and Sara took a week off before starting her volunteer work at a church in south Yonkers. For three hours every morning she would work with children from the public schools, one on one, to help them with reading. Many of them spoke English as a second language, and they needed reinforcement in it.

She was in her kitchen, looking at the church calendar that was tacked to the bulletin board. It was the last week of June now, and she idly leafed ahead to December, hoping to find a preview of January, when the baby was due.

There wasn't a preview, which she thought was strange. At the end of a calendar there was usually at least a glimpse of the following year.

At that moment the phone rang.

"Hello?" she said, afraid as usual that something had happened to her father.

"Hi." It was Becky.

"How are you doing?" she asked her sister, wondering if something had happened to her.

"I can't talk long, but I wanted to tell you—" There was a pause as if Becky were making sure that no one was listening, and then she said: "The deal's off."

"You're going to keep the baby?"

"No. I got rid of it," Becky said, and then she hung up.

TEN

TO MAKE SURE she had understood correctly, she tried calling her sister back, but she couldn't get past the secretary.

She hung up the phone, still in shock, still not believing what she had heard. She found her way to the kitchen table and sat down, still looking for another interpretation of what Becky had told her. But she kept hearing: "I got rid of it."

A wave of anger rose inside of her, swollen with the anger she had controlled over the years, from the destruction of her dolls through the vandalism of her yearbook to the betrayal of her confidence over Marcelo's situation. Not to mention her sister's triumphant announcement that she could have a baby with no problem.

It wasn't as if Sara had talked her sister into giving her the unwanted baby. Her sister had offered to give it to her. Before Sara could suggest it, her sister had come up with the solution, and her sister had made a deal with her.

As she wondered why Becky had broken the deal, her first thought was Bart. Her sister had been afraid to tell her husband that she was pregnant with another man's baby, or she had told him and he had flown into a rage, demanding that she get rid of it. So at least for a while Sara directed her anger at Bart, whom she had never liked anyway.

Then she faced the fact that it was Becky who had gotten rid of the baby. Bart hadn't done it, Becky had done it. Whatever Bart had told her to do, Becky was responsible for what she had done. And Becky had committed murder.

The magnitude of it turned Sara's anger away from her sister and toward the people who had helped Becky get rid of the baby. They were the ones who had committed murder.

She was still sitting at the kitchen table an hour later when she heard Marcelo enter the house.

Seeking comfort, she got up and went to meet him in the hall.

"What's wrong?" he asked, looking at her with concern.

"We lost our baby," she told him, beginning to cry.

"Did she have a miscarriage?"

"She had an abortion."

"Oh, no." Tenderly, he said: "*Ven aquí.*"

She went into his arms and pressed her face against his chest and sobbed her heart out.

He understood her well enough just to hold her and not say anything.

When she finally stopped crying she said: "I blame the people who did the abortion."

"You don't blame your sister?"

"I do blame her, but I blame them more. Without them she couldn't have done it."

"Let's sit down and talk about it."

They went to the sofa and sat down.

She lay back, feeling depressed.

Marcelo put his arm around her and took her hand. "Now, how do you know she had an abortion?"

"She called me and told me the deal was off. She said she got rid of the baby."

"That doesn't sound like a miscarriage."

"I knew what she meant. And then I wondered if I'd understood her correctly, so I called her back. But she wouldn't take my call."

"I wonder what made her change her mind."

"It could have been anything," Sara said. "It could have been Bart, or her career, or the thought of carrying a baby inside her for nine months—"

"Well, don't expect her to give you an explanation."

"Why not? She made a deal with me."

"But we knew there were problems," Marcelo said. "For one thing, she had to tell Bart."

"I have a feeling she never told him."

"If you're right, then you know why she did it."

"You mean to save her marriage."

"Why else?" He waited patiently for her to answer, giving her plenty of time to think.

"To stop me from having the baby."

"Now that you've said it, how do you feel?"

"I feel worse," Sara said. "I mean, how could I have such a thought about my sister?"

"You have some basis for it. From what I've seen and heard, your sister has always been envious of you."

"But to have an abortion—"

"I'm sorry she did it," Marcelo said. "But she has to live with it. You don't have to live with it."

"Yeah, I do. I have to live with the loss of a baby."

"A lot of women have to live with that. But there are other babies in the world. If your sister hadn't gotten pregnant, there wouldn't have been a baby to lose."

"But she did get pregnant."

"And she decided to have an abortion."

"Well, something must have driven her to do it. And I don't think it was Bart."

"You don't? If it wasn't Bart, then what was it?"

Sara hesitated. "Maybe it was me."

"It wasn't you. I mean, even if she did it to stop you from having the baby, it wasn't you who drove her to do it."

"I feel like it was."

"I know you do. But don't listen to that voice in your head. Listen to me," Marcelo said, taking her by the shoulders. "You're not responsible for what your sister did."

"I am if she was driven to do it by her feelings toward me."

"You're not responsible for her feelings."

"Not even if I made her have them?"

"You can't make another person have feelings. You can say things or do things, but they have choices on how to respond."

"What choice did Becky have?"

"She could have admired you instead of envying you."

"I guess she could have. I never realized that before. You know," she said, looking at him appreciatively, "you should have been a shrink."

He shook his head. "I'm better at being a family practitioner."

"You mean someone who knows a little about everything but not much about anything?"

They both laughed at her imitation of her father.

Talking with Marcelo had helped, but Sara still felt that her sister owed her an explanation, and she still blamed the people who had done the abortion. If her sister wouldn't explain why she had done it, then at least she could reveal who had done it.

Now that she was on summer recess she was free to have lunch with her sister on a weekday, so she called Becky's office the next morning with the hope of making an appointment. But she couldn't get past the secretary.

So she gave up on the idea of having lunch with her sister. She would see Becky anyway on the following Sunday, the Fourth of July. It was a family tradition to have a party on that holiday, and Sara was hosting it.

An hour later, as she was walking to Palisade Avenue to buy groceries, she saw Father Paul in front of the church. As usual he was blissfully smoking a cigarette.

"I hear your father's moving back to Woodlawn," the priest said after exhaling a long stream of smoke.

"He's planning to. We're looking for an apartment."

"That will decrease his commuting time."

"It will, but it will increase mine."

"Well, maybe you can find a double house and share it with him." A faint hint of mischief in Father Paul's eyes indicated that he was joking.

"Maybe we could. But then I'd have to commute back here to teach at the school."

"I guess you would. So maybe it's not such a good idea."

"I meant to ask you," Sara said, changing the subject. "Do

you know the monk who stands in front of the women's clinic in Dobbs Ferry?"

"You mean the guy in the white robe?"

"Is he really a monk?"

"He claims he is. He calls himself Brother Jeremiah."

"Jeremiah? What order is he?"

"His own order."

"So he's not a Catholic?"

"He used to be, but he split off and formed his own church. If you know the book of his namesake, you can guess what he believes in."

"I never read it. What's it about?"

"Retribution. Jeremiah was a prophet who spent his life warning the people of Israel about the wrath of God."

"Did they listen to him?"

"Evidently not. They were conquered by the Babylonians and taken away in captivity."

"What did they do to offend God?"

"They broke their covenant with Him," Father Paul said, "and they were worshiping other gods."

"So this monk, or whatever he is, believes in a vengeful god."

"His namesake gets pretty graphic. He tells people that if they don't change their ways, they'll be put to the sword and become meat for wild animals."

"That doesn't sound like the God I believe in."

"Well, the people of Israel were in a bad situation. Jeremiah must have figured that the only way to save them was to scare the living hell out of them."

"But it didn't work."

"It never works."

"What does work?"

"Love works."

"I know it does," Sara said, based on her own experience, "but it doesn't stop people from having abortions."

"If love doesn't stop them, fear won't either."

"The people who kill doctors at abortion clinics believe it'll stop them."

"They believe that if they kill some doctors, then other doctors will stop doing it?"

"I assume they do. Why else would they kill doctors?"

"They could believe they're doing God's work by punishing doctors who do abortions. That would justify killing them."

"Do you think this monk, Brother Jeremiah, believes he's doing God's work?"

"I'm sure he does. Like his namesake," Father Paul said, "he talks about how God will punish the doctors who do abortions. And maybe he'll try to prove he's a prophet."

"I can't understand why anyone would feel the need to do that. But I *can* understand why he would want to kill a doctor for other reasons."

"Can you give me an example?"

She didn't have to search far. "Suppose the doctor had done an abortion on his sister."

"If that happened, then he'd obviously have a personal reason for killing the doctor."

"So he'd be doing it for revenge."

"That's what it sounds like."

"Could he still believe he's doing God's work?"

"Oh, yes. He could. But he'd be wrong."

"I know," she said, responding to the hint of concern in the priest's eyes.

Back at the apartment she found Becky at the dining table having a solitary meal.

Becky didn't look up from her plate, and she didn't say anything. She just kept eating, mechanically putting food into her mouth and deliberately chewing.

Sara sat down opposite her sister and confronted her, asking: "Why did you tell mom that Marcelo's married?"

"She asked me about him," Becky said after swallowing.

"You didn't have to tell her he's married."

"I didn't want to lie to her."

"Did she ask if he was married?"

"No. She didn't. But there are sins of omission as well as sins of commission."

"You mean if you hadn't told her Marcelo was married, even though she didn't ask, you would have been *lying* to her?"

Becky took another bite of food, chewed, and swallowed. "Of course I would have."

"That's bullshit," Sara said. "You told her because you wanted to make trouble for me."

"Why would I want to make trouble for you?"

"I don't know why. I can't imagine doing that to you."

"You mean you can't imagine not lying to mom?"

"We're not talking about lying to mom."

"Then what are we talking about?"

"We're talking about why you want to make trouble for me."

"I don't want to make trouble for you. So there's nothing to talk about."

"Well, that's the last time I ever share a confidence with you. I can't trust you."

"You're asking too much," Becky said with her fork poised over the plate, "if you expect me to lie to mom to cover up what you're doing. I have a relationship with mom, and it's based on that fact that I don't lie to her."

"I have a relationship with her too, and I only lie to her so she won't worry."

"I don't ever lie to her."

"You don't have anything to lie about." She immediately felt bad for saying this since it was hurtful, and she didn't want to hurt her sister, she only wanted her sister to stop hurting her. "I'm sorry. I didn't mean that."

"If you hadn't meant it, you wouldn't have said it."

"All right. I meant it. I'm sorry."

"The only thing I have is my relationship with mom. And you want me to ruin it by lying to her."

"I don't want to ruin your relationship with mom."

"You do," Becky said with tears forming. "You want me to sacrifice the only thing I have just to cover up the fact that you're going out with a married man and spending the night with him and fucking him."

"I'm not fucking him," Sara insisted, "I'm making love with him. There's a difference."

"Whatever you're doing, I'm tired of covering up for you. The next time mom calls on a Sunday morning I'm going to tell her where you are."

"Go ahead and tell her. I had a good talk with her, and she understands."

"I bet she doesn't know you're fucking him."

"I don't know what she knows. And I'm not fucking him."

"Then you shouldn't mind if I tell her the truth."

"I don't mind. You can tell her anything you want."

"Okay. I will." Her sister resumed eating.

Sara watched her sister for a while, looking for a way to break the impasse. "If you're committed to telling the truth, then you should tell *me* the truth."

"The truth about what?"

"The truth about our relationship."

"There's nothing to tell. You're daddy's little girl, and I'm not the boy he wanted."

"You don't really believe that, do you?"

"How could I not believe it?"

"But I don't get any special attention from him."

"You do. You get all his attention."

"I never noticed. I always thought he treated us equally."

"He doesn't treat us equally. He pays attention to you, and he ignores me."

"Well, maybe that's because you ignore him."

"I don't ignore him."

"You're so fixed on mom, you don't pay any attention to him."

"Why should I pay attention to him," Becky asked, "if he doesn't pay attention to me?"

"Someone has to go first."

"The parent should go first."

"Parents are human, just like us."

"They're still supposed to lead the way."

"They usually do, but sometimes they don't. So the truth about our relationship," Sara said after a silence, "is that you envy my relationship with dad."

"I don't envy your relationship with daddy."

"I just heard you say I'm daddy's little girl, and you're not the boy he wanted. If that isn't envy, what the hell is it?"

"It's a feeling of injustice."

"I'll accept that. So you feel that after doing better than I did at everything, you should get more recognition from him."

"That's how I feel," Becky admitted.

"I'm sorry. But if you do things only to get recognition for them, you're always going to be disappointed."

"I don't do things only to get recognition for them."

"Well, if it's partly why you do them, you're still going to be disappointed."

"Then why should I do them?"

"You should do them because you like doing them, and also because you're good at doing them."

"Do you like your job?"

"I like it enough, and I'm good enough at it. But I don't see myself doing it forever."

"So what do you see yourself doing?"

"Teaching school," Sara said. "When I was younger I wanted to be a teacher, just like Sister Laura. And then for some reason I stopped wanting to be a teacher. But now I'm coming back to it. I guess I wasn't ready before."

"You'd make a good teacher," Becky said.

"I value your opinion," Sara said.

There was a long silence.

"All right," Becky said. "I'll keep covering up for you. But how long will it take Marcelo to get an annulment?"

"Not much longer. And thanks. I don't want mom to worry."

The following Saturday she went to the Bronx to meet Marcelo's mother, who had gathered some members of the extended family for a party.

His mother was a solid woman with a face that expressed serenity. Though she had at least twenty guests for the party, she acted as if everything would happen of its own accord, and whenever a daughter, a sister, or a niece approached her with a potential problem, she would take it in stride and happily say: "*No hay problema.*"

His sister Rosa brought two little children who were adorable, and Sara spent some time with them, imagining the children she would have with Marcelo.

She also spent some time in the kitchen with his mother, who had prepared a magnificent feast of Dominican dishes, including *pastelitos* and *sancocho*.

"I do not speak English well," his mother told her.

"*No hay problema,*" Sara said. "*No hablo bién el español.*"

"You speak Spanish?" his mother said, staring at Sara as if a cat had just talked.

"*No mucho,* but we can manage. Could I have the recipe for your *sancocho?*"

"It's not written down. I got it from my mother. But I can tell you what goes into it. You start with a *sofrito*—"

Sara got out her notebook and wrote down the ingredients and the steps.

At the table sitting between two of Marcelo's sisters she felt completely welcome. They all seemed to accept her without the kind of questions that her family asked. The only questions they did ask were about her family.

"You only have one sister?" Rosa asked.

"One's enough," she said, smiling.

"One sister wouldn't be enough for me. I like having three sisters."

"Would you have liked to have a brother?" Alma asked.

"I guess I would have. Do you like having brothers?"

"I like having brothers to protect me."

"Are they good at that?"

"They are. You should have seen Marcelo when some guys tried to hassle me. Remember, Rosa?"

"Yeah, I remember. There were three big guys. And when Marcelo was done with them, they ran away like beach dogs."

"What did he do to them?" Sara asked, not having imagined this side of Marcelo.

"The biggest guy came after him," Alma said, "and Marcelo gave him a chop in the neck, which made him gasp for breath."

"And then the other two guys came after him," Rosa said. "He kicked the first guy in the *cojones*, and he kicked the second guy in the *culo*."

"You know what *cojones* are, don't you?" Alma said.

"Oh, yeah. I do," Sara said. "And I know what a *culo* is."

"The second guy turned to run away, so that's why Marcelo kicked him in the *culo*," Rosa explained.

"He saw what had happened to the other two guys," Alma said with sibling pride.

"We don't want to give the wrong impression," Rosa said. "Marcelo's the kindest, gentlest man in the whole world. But he can be tough when he needs to be."

"Was he ever tough with you?" Sara asked jokingly.

"When we acted like sluts he was," Alma said.

She gazed at Marcelo, appreciating this other side of him. Marcelo, oblivious of her, was busy eating *sancocho* and talking with an uncle.

By the end of July, when it looked as if Marcelo would get the annulment in September, she contacted the priest at St. Barnabas and set a date for the wedding in October. She was cutting it close, but all things considered, she preferred the risk that Marcelo wouldn't get the annulment in time to the risk that she would get pregnant before the wedding.

Of course she tried to avoid making love at the times when she was likely to conceive, but you never knew exactly when those times were, and you never knew exactly when you were going to make love.

By the grace of God, the annulment came through at the end of September, and they were married three weeks later.

According to everyone who attended, the wedding was beautiful and the reception was a great party. With all the people her parents knew and Marcelo's extended family, there were at least two hundred guests, and in order to accommodate all of them her father rented a hall at Villa Barone, a famous place for wedding receptions in the Bronx.

When the time came for her to dance with her father the band started playing "Daddy's Little Girl." She had asked them not to, remembering what Becky had said, but they followed tradition and did it anyway.

As she moved around the floor with her father, who was a good dancer and led her with style, though he was already three sheets to the wind, she enjoyed being his little girl, at least for this moment, and she hoped that Becky would have the same experience.

During most of the dinner the band played standard popular songs, with an occasional Irish song, but as dessert was coming around the band broke into a Latin beat, and all the people on Marcelo's side got up to dance.

The first number was a *merengue*, which Marcelo had taught her, so they got up and joined the crowd of exuberant Latinos on the dance floor.

Dancing with Marcelo, she admired the way he held his upper body still and moved only his hips and legs to the rhythm of the music. They were as close together as her wedding dress would allow, and they were giving their bodies free rein.

"Not bad," Alma told her, sliding by. "You dance like a real Dominican."

Sara smiled. Of all the compliments she received that day, this was the best one.

Becky and Bart were late for the party on the Fourth of July. They were so late that Sara was about to call them and make sure they were coming when they finally arrived. Of course she understood why Becky wouldn't want to see her, but sooner or later they had to talk.

The opportunity came while Becky was in the kitchen helping her clean up and the men were out on the porch talking about the Yankees.

"How are you doing?" Sara asked, rinsing a plate.

"Not well," Becky said, standing next to her.

"You haven't told me exactly what happened."

"You don't want to know."

"I do want to know."

"I went to a clinic," Becky admitted. "I only went there for a consultation, but I ended up having an abortion."

"Are you saying it happened without your consent?"

"No. I consented to it. But I didn't know what I was doing."

"Why did you go to a clinic for a consultation? You have a doctor, don't you?"

"Yes. But I wanted a second opinion."

"On what? On whether the baby was all right?"

"I don't know," her sister sighed.

"So what happened?"

"The doctor examined me, and then he asked me if I wanted the baby—"

"He asked you that? Why?"

"I don't know. Maybe he could tell I didn't want it."

"What did you say?"

"I said I didn't want the baby."

"And what did he say?"

"He explained that I had a choice in the matter. If I didn't want the baby, then I could have an abortion. It was safe, and it was legal."

"Did he say it was moral?"

"He said it was up to me to decide if it was right."

"It's not up to you," Sara didn't say. Instead, she asked: "And what did you decide?"

"I decided it was right to save my marriage."

"What about the deal you made with me?"

"I only made it because I didn't think I had any choice."

"So when the doctor explained that you did have a choice, you found another solution."

"I did. And let's be honest," Becky said. "It never would have worked for you to raise my baby. It would have been bad for all of us, including the baby."

Sara stared into the sink. "You mean it would have been worse for the baby than not being born?"

"At times I wish I'd never been born."

Without looking at her, Sara knew that her sister had begun to cry, and she felt bad, but she couldn't stop herself from saying: "But at times aren't you glad you *were* born?"

"I don't know. I guess I am."

There were other things she would have liked to say, but she didn't want to beat up on her sister. "So the doctor did the abortion on the spot?"

"Another doctor did it."

"They didn't advise you to think about it?"

"I didn't need to think about it."

"How could they have known that?"

"I told them," Becky said, reaching for the plate that Sara was holding in suspension.

"Didn't they ask how your husband felt about it?"

"I told them he didn't know about it. They understood."

"I bet they did. They must have seen a lot of women in that situation. So they went ahead and killed my baby."

"It wasn't your baby, it was my baby," Becky said with rising emotion. "And I had a right to do whatever I thought was best."

"You didn't have a right to end that baby's life."

"I did. I had a legal right."

"You didn't have a moral right."

"Don't give me that. Those celibate old men in Rome have no idea what it's like to be a woman. They have no right to tell us what's moral."

"If you know better than they do, then tell me—" Sara said, turning to her sister. "Is it moral to end an old person's life? Is it moral to end a sick person's life? Is it moral to end a disabled person's life? Is it moral to end an unhappy person's life?"

"I don't know," Becky said, beginning to wail. "I just know it was right for me."

At that moment Bart came into the kitchen.

"What's wrong?" he asked, looking at Becky.

"Nothing," Becky said, wiping her eyes.

"Did she say something to hurt you?"

Becky shook her head.

Bart turned on Sara. "Why do you always make her cry?"

"I don't make her cry," Sara said. "And anyway, it's none of your business."

"It *is* my business," Bart told her, raising his voice in anger. "Becky's my wife."

"You're being ridiculous," Sara said, reaching for a plate.

"When I talk to you, I expect you to listen."

"Why should I listen? You have nothing to say."

"You have no right to talk to me that way," Bart roared. He gave her a hard push on the shoulder, making her drop the plate and fall to the floor.

Sara looked up at him, wanting to kill him.

Becky reached down to help her up.

"What the hell happened?" Marcelo asked, appearing in the kitchen doorway.

Remembering what his sisters had said about him, Sara was tempted to tell him what had happened and see what he would do to Bart, but she overcame the impulse.

"Nothing," she said, starting to get up off the floor. "I just lost my balance."

"Are you all right?"

"Yeah. I'm fine."

"We have to go now," Bart said, taking command. He didn't apologize for what he had done.

Before leaving, Becky asked: "Are you all right?"

"Yeah, what about you?"

"I'm so sorry," Becky said, seeking a hug and finding it.

"I don't blame you," Sara said, gently rubbing her sister's back. "I blame them."

ELEVEN

WHEN MARCELO returned from taking her father home he joined her on the porch, where she was sitting with a glass of white wine. The sun was over the Palisades now but still high enough so that it didn't shine under the awning and into her eyes.

"You didn't just lose your balance," Marcelo said, sitting down next to her. He had stopped in the kitchen to pour himself a glass of rum, which he always drank *sin hielo.*

"Bart pushed me," Sara admitted. "I didn't want to tell you at the time."

"I could tell from the way you were looking at him that Bart had done something to you. Why did he push you?"

"He was playing the role of a husband who protects his wife."

"And you didn't want me to play that role."

"Not at the time. There was already enough going on."

Marcelo sipped his rum. "I assume that Becky told you what she did with the baby."

"Yeah. She told me." Sara grimly related what Becky had told her, putting the blame more on the clinic than on her sister and ending with the statement: "They killed our baby."

"They did kill it. But it wasn't our baby."

"It *was* our baby. My sister agreed to give it to us."

"So your sister changed her mind," Marcelo said as if it were perfectly understandable.

"*They* changed her mind," Sara said. "They talked her into it. They wanted the fee."

"They couldn't have talked her into doing something she didn't want to do already. She went to the clinic on her own volition. No one forced her to go there."

"I think she was driven to go there."

"If she was, she was driven by her own feelings, not by anything you said or did."

"But they shouldn't have done it on the spot. They should have advised her to think it over and to come back if she wanted to go through with it."

"Are you sure they didn't?"

"She said they didn't."

"Well, maybe she's trying to avoid taking responsibility for what she did by blaming someone else. It wouldn't be the first time your sister did that."

"You mean she might not have told me the whole truth?"

"She could have left out some vital information."

"There are sins of omission as well as sins of commission," Sara quoted her sister, wondering if her husband was right.

"It does seem a little unusual that a woman would walk into a clinic and ten minutes later have an abortion."

"That isn't what they do?"

"No. They give the woman a chance to think about it."

"So she could have gone for a consultation and thought about it and then gone back?"

"She could have. And I understand why she would have left that part out."

"Well, even if she did go back, I still blame them. She didn't kill the baby, they did."

"Whatever they did, they did with her consent."

"But she was desperate. She didn't know what she was doing. And they took advantage of her situation."

"They didn't take advantage of it," Marcelo said. "They offered her a solution, and she decided it was better than the solution you offered her."

"You mean better for her, but not for the baby."

"She wasn't thinking about the baby, except as a problem."

"But it was alive, it was a gift from God."

"It was," he agreed, reaching out and taking her hand. "And we have a right to grieve for it. But then we have to accept what happened, so we can move on."

She knew he was right, but she was far from accepting what had happened. She tightened her grip on his hand, and with her other hand she shielded her eyes from the sun, which had begun to shine under the awning.

Two days later when she went to the Korean grocery store she left her car in the parking lot and walked up the street to the women's clinic.

As usual there was a group of protesters on the sidewalk holding up signs, and among them she saw Brother Jeremiah. He was an attractive man, and the closer she got to him the more she felt the power of his charisma.

He moved forward to meet her, saying: "We're here to help you, sister."

"I'm not going to the clinic," she told him. "I came here to learn more about you."

"Are you from the press?" he asked hopefully.

"No, I'm only an individual who supports what you're doing."

"You do? That's great. But why do you support us?"

"I'm a Catholic, and I support the position of my church."

"I used to be a Catholic, but I've moved beyond that. I didn't think the church was active enough in opposing abortion."

"Well, maybe I haven't been active enough."

"You're welcome to join us. We're here every day."

"I might join you. But let me ask you," Sara said, "suppose I *had* been going to the clinic, what would you have done?"

"If you were intending to have an abortion, I would have tried to stop you."

"But how would you know if I was intending to have an abortion?"

"I would have known by looking at you."

"You didn't know by looking at me. I mean, you told me you were here to help me."

"I could see you were in trouble," Brother Jeremiah said with compassion in his eyes. "But you didn't look like a woman who intended to have an abortion."

"What did I look like?"

"You looked like a woman who regretted having an abortion."

"If that was my situation, then why would I be going back to the clinic?"

"To tell them they did a terrible thing."

"You're right about how I feel. But you're wrong about my situation. I didn't have an abortion. My sister did."

"It's almost the same situation," he said. "The only difference is that instead of killing your son or daughter, they killed your nephew or niece."

"They killed my son or daughter," she didn't say, feeling she had told this man enough. "But if I *had* come here to have an abortion, how would you have tried to stop me?"

"I would have told you that abortion is murder, and that murder is a deadly sin."

"Does that stop people?"

"It stops some people. It wakes them up to what they're about to do."

"But it doesn't stop other people."

"It doesn't stop atheists. And it doesn't stop people who have a strong reason for not wanting to have a baby."

"If my sister had come here to have an abortion," Sara said after reflecting, "I wonder if you could have stopped her."

"I would have tried."

"I would have too. But I didn't know she was even thinking about an abortion."

"So you feel you should have stopped her."

"I do. I feel responsible."

"Well, there's nothing you can do about your sister. But there *is* something you can do about these other women."

Sara understood. "You mean I can join your group here?"

"Yes. And maybe there's something more you could do," the monk said, looking at her speculatively. "How do you feel about doctors who do abortions?"

"I feel angry at them. I can understand why people want to kill them. I never thought I would understand, but I do now."

Brother Jeremiah nodded with approval. "Then you could be a valuable member of our group. If you're free tomorrow, come back and join us. And make yourself a sign."

"I will. I'm free for the rest of the summer."

They were at her parent's house for Thanksgiving. Sara and her mother were having coffee at the kitchen table, Becky was taking a nap in the bedroom they used to share, and the men were in the living room watching a football game.

"I wanted to tell you," her mother said. "Your father and I have decided to sell this house."

"You have? Why?"

"It's too much for us."

"I can understand why *you* might want to sell this house, but I can't imagine dad wanting to sell it. He grew up in this house. He's spent his whole life here."

"He's tired of being a landlord. He had to give notice to our tenants. They don't take care of things, and they don't pay the rent on time."

"So you want to live in a smaller house?"

"That's right. A one-family house."

"Will you buy a house in this neighborhood?"

"We haven't decided that yet," her mother said. "But I don't want to stay in Woodlawn."

"Why not?"

"I feel like I'm still a stranger here. Your father has his old friends, but my old friends are over in Yonkers. And we don't see the parents of your friends because now that you're grown up, we no longer have any reason to see them."

"So where would you go?"

"We'd go to my old neighborhood."

"Well, I don't blame you," Sara said, "but I can't imagine dad leaving Woodlawn."

"If we lived in Yonkers, he could drive back here every day to see his friends."

"What church would you go to?"

"We'd still go to St. Barnabas. I might be able to talk him into going to St. Brigid now and then, but I know the limits."

"How long have you lived in Woodlawn?"

"Thirty years. For all these years I've done what your father wanted, and now it's my turn."

"I think it is," Sara said, siding with her mother.

"I haven't told Becky about this yet. You know how she is. She'll be against it, and she'll get very emotional about it."

"She won't want you to sell the house where she grew up."

"If she wants to keep it, she can buy it from us."

Sara laughed. "I can't imagine her buying it. I think she'll want you to keep it for her."

"Well, she wouldn't want to live in Woodlawn. It doesn't have enough status."

Sara refrained from commenting. "What about the tenants? You said that dad gave them notice."

"We hope they leave," her mother said. "If the house is empty, it'll be easier to sell."

"It should be. The new owners can find their own tenants. Or they can share the house with their parents."

"We did that for twenty years." Her mother didn't have to say: "And that was enough."

"You said you haven't decided where you'll buy a house," Sara said after a moment. "I guess that means dad hasn't agreed to leave Woodlawn."

"No, he hasn't. I'm still working on him."

"If you think it would help, I'll work on him too."

"I was hoping you would. You have some influence on him."

"I do? He never listens to me."

"He always listens to you."

That was a revelation to Sara, though it conformed with Becky's accusation that she was daddy's little girl. "Okay. I'll use whatever influence I have."

She never knew to what extent she had influenced her father, but six months later her parents sold the house in Woodlawn and bought a house in Yonkers. Her father began his daily commute back to Woodlawn, and they continued to attend St. Barnabas. Her mother didn't mind these arrangements since now she lived close to her old friends.

But less than a year after they moved, Sara got a phone call at work from her father.

"Your mother's gone," he said in a panic.

"What do you mean?" She didn't think he meant that her mother had left him, especially after he had just moved to Yonkers to make her happy, but she didn't want to believe the alternative.

"I found her on the kitchen floor when I got back from Woodlawn. I called the police, and they took her to the hospital. The doctor said she had a massive heart attack."

"Did she die?"

"Yes. She passed away."

"Oh, God," she said as it hit her.

"I'm at the hospital. I don't want to leave her."

"Well, stay there until we get there."

"I will," her father said almost docilely.

She called Marcelo at the clinic and told him what had happened. They agreed that he should drive to the hospital directly from the Bronx and that she should take the train to the Glenwood station, which was within walking distance from the hospital.

She had trouble reaching her sister at work, but she finally did. When she told her what had happened she had to wait for a long time while Becky went into hysterics. They agreed to meet at Grand Central.

She found her sister standing forlornly in the vast space of the main hall. She took Becky into her arms and held her.

"Mom was the only thing I had," her sister sobbed. "And now I have nothing."

"You have me, and you have dad."

"I have nothing," her sister didn't have to repeat.

Through the wake and the funeral and the burial she thanked God that she had Marcelo, and she shared him with her father and her sister. She didn't see how they could have gotten through that ordeal without him.

The weekend after the funeral they went to Yonkers to check on her father. They found him at home in his lounger with a bottle of Jameson on the table. They learned that he hadn't left the house since the funeral, not even to go to Woodlawn.

Sara straightened up the house while Marcelo got her father to shower and change his clothes. They took him out to dinner at a new restaurant on Executive Boulevard, but he hardly touched his food. She had never seen her father leave so much food on his plate. It was enough for two doggie bags.

On the way back to the city they agreed that they should move to Yonkers so that they could take care of her father.

A few months after they moved, Becky met Bart, and six months later she married him. By then Sara and Marcelo were living in Yonkers, her father had resumed his daily commute to Woodlawn, and Sara had begun a master's program in education at St. Catherine, which was conveniently located across Odell Avenue from the hospital.

Since Bart had been married before, Becky had her wedding at an Episcopal church in Yonkers and her reception at a place on the river. Sara later learned that Bart had absolutely refused to hold either of these events in the Bronx.

Her father had heard that the ground floor of a two-family house on the street where they had lived in Woodlawn was available for rent, and he asked her to go and look at it with him. She had to drive his Crown Victoria since he refused to ride in her Honda, but she quickly got the hang of the larger car, and she even managed to squeeze it into a parking spot that didn't look big enough to her eye but did to her father's eye.

"Not a bad job of parking," her father didn't have to say.

The house resembled their old house, and her father thought it could have been built by the same contractor. The main difference was that instead of a front lawn and a hedge there was a paved area and a wrought-iron fence, and everything was perfectly maintained.

"They must be Italian," her father said.

"You don't know their name?"

"I only got the address. I didn't want to talk with anyone before seeing the house."

"So what if no one's home?"

"Then we'll come back."

She rang the bell for the upper floor, and within a few minutes a woman about her age opened the door, looking as if she were ready to deal with a couple of evangelicals.

"We heard you have an apartment to rent," Sara told her.

"Yeah," the woman said. "Would you like to see it?"

"If it's no trouble." Sara introduced her father and herself, explaining that her father was the one who was interested in the apartment, and then they followed the woman, whose name was Gioia, through the other front door.

"My husband's mother lived here," Gioia said.

That explained the floral scent that greeted them, which if her father lived here would be replaced by a tobacco scent.

The rooms, which were devoid of furniture, were immaculate.

Sara could see that her father liked the apartment, and she could imagine him living here, so they began to discuss the terms of a rental agreement.

"We have a rule," Gioia said. "No smoking in the house."

Sara expected a negative reaction from her father, but he just nodded as if that wouldn't be a problem. He had, after all, learned to obey that rule in her house.

Luckily, they didn't have a rule against cats.

They left after making a verbal agreement and headed for Monahan's, which of course was within walking distance.

For a weekday noon the place was lively. A tall lanky man was standing at the bar, ordering another round of drinks for everyone.

"What's the occasion?" Sara asked a happy bystander. "Did he win the lottery?"

"He just had his second grandson."

At that moment the man held up two fingers as if he were making a sign of victory.

"Let's drink to number two," another man said.

"And number three, and number four," another man said.

She followed her father to a booth, where they sat down and waited for their free drink.

"So when am I going to have a grandson?" her father asked.

"When God decides to give you one," Sara replied.

"He's sure taking a long time."

"Actually, I have something to tell you—" She paused only long enough to catch her breath and brace herself for her father's reaction since she didn't want to raise any false hopes. "Marcelo and I have decided to adopt a baby."

"You mean you've given up?"

"We haven't given up. But while we're waiting for a miracle, we want to be parents. We want to raise children."

"You do, uh. What kind of baby would you get?"

"A baby who needs a mother and father."

"Well, I don't want to have a Jap grandson."

"I don't think there are Japanese children available to adopt."

"You know what I mean," her father said. "I want a grandson who looks like me."

"Do you want a granddaughter who looks like you?"

"No. I want a granddaughter who looks like you."

"I'll see what we can get," she said, smiling.

Their free drinks arrived, a pint of Guinness for her father and a white wine for her.

"And what the hell is your sister doing?"

"What do you mean?"

"Why isn't she pregnant?"

"I don't know." The lie came easily. There was absolutely no reason for her father to know what had happened. Of all the lies she had told her mother, none had been so necessary to protect a parent from the truth.

"You know what the problem is? You're spending too much time at computers."

"What do computers have to do with it?"

"They send out cathode rays that sterilize you."

Sara laughed. "Cathode rays? They sound like something out of science fiction."

"They're not science fiction," her father said as if he had been involved in discovering them. "They're emitted from the tubes of televisions and computers."

"Well, I'm not sterile," Sara said. "My problem is, my uterus isn't hospitable for fertilized eggs."

"That's what your doctors tell you, but they don't know shit. You problem is exposure to cathode rays."

Sara didn't argue with his theory since it deflected the blame from her to something else.

The next day she joined the group of protesters in front of the clinic holding a sign that said: "They murdered my baby."

When she had finished making the sign she showed it to Marcelo. It was on the kitchen table, ready to be attached to a pole that she had bought along with the cardboard.

"It's true," he said, looking concerned. "The doctor who performed that operation on your sister did murder what you thought was your baby, but why do you want to say it in public?"

"I want to get it out. If I keep it inside me, it'll poison me."

"I understand. And I don't have a problem as long as you're not calling for retribution."

"I'm not calling for retribution," Sara assured him. "I just want to stop them from killing babies."

"What if your protests don't stop them?"

"I don't know. I haven't thought it through that far."

"At some point you'll have to think it through because your protests won't stop them."

"I think I'll know when I've reached that point."

"Good. Just tell me when you do."

"I will. Don't worry."

She was greeted warmly by Brother Jeremiah, who liked her sign, and he stood by her during most of her first day of protest.

On her second day a young woman on her way into the clinic stopped and asked her: "Did you have an abortion?"

"No. I didn't. The woman who was carrying my baby did."

"Was she your surrogate?"

"She was my sister."

"Then how could it have been your baby?"

"She told me I could have it."

"That makes my situation look simple. I got pregnant by accident, and I don't want to have the baby. I'm not married, and I'm not ready to be a parent."

"How do you know you're not ready?"

"I don't feel ready. There're things I want to do before I get tied down with children."

"What things?"

"I want to make money, I want to live in a nice apartment, I want to travel—"

Sara waited to hear more, but the young woman had already run out of things she wanted to do before she got tied down with children. "I can tell you from experience that for those things I wouldn't give up having children."

"I'm not giving up having children. I just don't want to have this baby."

"What if you can't have another baby?"

"My doctor recommended this clinic," the woman said as if she didn't want to consider the possibility of anything going wrong. "They know what they're doing."

"I wonder," Sara said. "I wonder if they have any idea what they're doing."

The woman gave her a worried look. "Well, I only came here for a consultation. I haven't made a decision."

"Good. Don't let them talk you into it."

As she watched the young woman go into the clinic she hoped they wouldn't talk her into it. But she didn't feel that she had talked her out of it.

"You handled that well," Brother Jeremiah said. "But you can see what we're up against. They always have the last word."

"They wouldn't have the last word if we stopped the women from going in there."

"Words aren't enough for most of them. You have to stop them physically."

"You tried that, didn't you?"

"We tried it once. And they called the police, who came and arrested us. It gave us some publicity, but that's all."

"How else could you stop them?"

"If you want to take a break, I'll tell you how."

They walked across the street to a neighborhood store, where Brother Jeremiah bought her a coffee. They went to the hillside that overlooked the village swimming pool. When they sat down, she noticed that he was wearing jeans under his robe.

The children were getting in and out of the pool, splashing around in the sunlit water, and doing just about everything except swimming.

"As we sit here," Brother Jeremiah said, "they're killing a baby who years from now could be playing in that pool."

She imagined her sister's baby playing in the pool. "So how could you stop them?"

"By destroying the clinic."

"How would you destroy it?"

"By blowing it up."

"How would you avoid hurting people?"

"By timing the bomb to go off at three in the morning."

She realized that he wasn't just talking, he had worked out a plan in detail. And she felt an involuntary thrill at the idea of blowing up the clinic. But immediately she had concerns. "What if there was a cleaning woman in the building?"

"We know their schedule. They finish at ten."

"Well, what about a security guard?"

"They don't have a security guard. They lock the building and turn on an alarm system."

"If there's an alarm system, you couldn't get into the building at night to plant the bomb."

"I know we couldn't. We'd plant the bomb during the day."

"How would you do that?"

"A woman, pretending to be a patient, would walk in with the bomb in her handbag. Instead of going to the reception desk, she'd go directly into the bathroom and lock the door. There's a cabinet under the sink where they store toilet paper and towels. She'd hide the bomb in the cabinet behind the supplies. She'd stay there long enough so if people noticed her leaving the bathroom, they wouldn't remember where she came from. And she'd walk out as if she were finished with her consultation."

"How would she carry a bomb in her handbag?"

"These bombs are made of plastic. They're small and light."

"What about the timer?"

"The timer is digital, and it has a miniature battery. It would fit easily into a handbag."

"But why would a woman do that for you?"

"She wouldn't be doing it for me, she'd be doing it for God. He wants us to destroy this clinic."

"If God wants the clinic destroyed, then why doesn't He strike it with a bolt of lightning?"

"That's not how God does things," Brother Jeremiah said. "He relies on us to do His work."

Sara resisted. "I know it's only a building, but destroying the clinic would be an act of violence, and my religion is against violence."

"Where did you get that idea?"

"It's what they taught me."

"Well, they didn't give you the full story. Did they tell you what Jesus said to his disciples? He said: 'I come not to bring peace, but to bring a sword.' Did they tell you that?"

"I remember it. But they said He didn't mean it literally. They said He meant the word of God, not a sword."

"He meant a sword. He wasn't against using weapons. How do you think He drove the merchants and the bankers out of the temple?"

"That was a temple. This is a clinic."

"It's a temple of death. The people who work there have offended God, and if it weren't for the intercession of Jesus, do you know how God would punish them?"

She didn't have a chance to say: "No. How?"

"He'd have them all put to the sword, and He'd let hyenas feed on their corpses. But thanks to the intercession of Jesus, He won't destroy them. He'll only destroy their temple of death. He won't kill them. He'll only stop them from killing others."

"So you'd be doing God's work by destroying the clinic?"

"I'd be doing what Jesus did at the temple."

"But you need a woman to carry out your plan."

"I found one," Brother Jeremiah said. "She's angry at the people who murdered her baby, but she's a Christian, and that stops her from murdering them. She's now at the point where she doesn't want revenge against them, she only wants to stop them from killing others. Destroying the clinic would give her an outlet for her anger, and she'd be doing God's work."

"You don't mean me," Sara said, unwilling to recognize herself from his description.

"I do mean you. I knew from the moment I first saw you that you were the one. And you have an advantage over the other women in the group. You just joined us, so when you walk into the clinic you won't be recognized as a protester."

As she felt herself being carried away by this man's purpose she could understand how her sister might have been talked into having an abortion.

"I'll have the bomb for you tomorrow. I'll meet you at this spot, and while we're having coffee I can transfer the bomb into your handbag."

"I haven't agreed to do it," she said, still resisting.

"You haven't said you won't do it," Brother Jeremiah said, casting his hypnotic eyes on her. "So I'm going to assume that you will do it."

TWELVE

WHEN SARA GOT home she brought in the mail, which consisted mostly of bills and catalogs, and she set it on the kitchen table. She checked the cupboard where she kept the pasta to make sure that she had linguine and canned tomatoes, which she needed for dinner. But she was low on Parmesan cheese, so she added that to her grocery list.

After putting away some dishes she went out onto the porch and gazed at the Palisades, wishing that God would give her a sign. When she was listening to Brother Jeremiah she was almost convinced that by bombing the clinic she would be doing God's work. But now, out of range of his charisma, she was almost convinced that it would be wrong—until she thought about all the babies they were killing.

Later, on the way to her father's house, she saw Father Paul in front of the church, and she felt a need to tell him about the bomb plot and get his guidance. But she had to make her own decision since she would have to live with it, so she only exchanged greetings with the priest and kept walking.

Her father wasn't home. She assumed he had taken a taxi over to Woodlawn, and he was in Monahan's celebrating his expected return to the old neighborhood. In his absence she was free to look around the house, identifying the major problems she would have to resolve before putting it on the market. The real estate agent that she had engaged was coming over the next morning to make an assessment, and Sara wanted to be ready for it.

Clearly, the worst problem was the fact that after five years of smoking cigars inside the house, which her mother hadn't permitted, her father had coated the walls and the ceilings of the downstairs rooms with a brownish film, creating the effects of a photograph in sepia. Of course the furniture smelled like smoke, but that would be moved to his apartment, provided that it slipped by the noses of the landlords. The new owners would want to replace the wall-to-wall carpet, which had brown stains that must have resulted from her father, acting as if he was out on the sidewalk, grinding out a cigar butt with the heel of his shoe. The smoke-coated walls and ceiling would have to be cleaned and then painted.

Another problem was the toilet in the powder room. The cover of the flush tank had been broken, accidentally dropped when her father removed it to adjust the float, and cemented together. It hadn't been replaced because her father hadn't been able to find a cover in a color that matched the toilet and sink, which they weren't making in pink anymore.

After leaving her father's house she walked over to Barca Brothers and bought the things she needed for dinner and breakfast. And then she walked home, passing the church, where people were arriving for the five o'clock mass. She knew that Father Paul would be celebrating that mass, and she felt a need to go into the church, but if she did then Marcelo would get home and wonder where she was, so she kept walking.

That evening there were times when she almost told Marcelo about the plot, but she didn't tell him. She had to make her own decision.

She lay awake through most of the night, with the alternating voices of Brother Jeremiah and her mother in her head. They pushed her and pulled her back and forth as if she were an object in a game between them.

"I come not to bring peace, but to bring a sword," Brother Jeremiah said.

"He came to bring love, not violence," her mother said.

"He won't kill them," Sara argued. "He'll only stop them from killing babies."

"What if the bomb doesn't go off when it's supposed to?"

"I knew from the moment I first saw you," Brother Jeremiah said, "that you were the one."

"He's using you for his own purpose."

When the dawn finally came she was still awake, and she still hadn't made a decision.

Her appointment with the real estate agent was at ten. They were meeting at her father's house, and Sara didn't want to keep the woman waiting, so she arrived ten minutes early.

The agent arrived precisely at ten. She was a rangy woman with red hair and glasses on a cord around her neck. She had her office on Palisade Avenue, so she knew the neighborhood. Her name was Peggy.

"Whew!" Peggy exclaimed upon entering the house. "It smells like a smokehouse."

"It does," Sara admitted, smiling.

"He could have hung sausages from the curtain rods and cured them."

"I don't know how they would have tasted."

"They would have tasted like cigar smoke—the quintessential male aroma."

"Well, I plan to clean the walls and ceilings and then paint them," Sara said.

"I wouldn't advise doing that yourself," Peggy said, looking at the ceiling. "I can give you a team of professionals who will come in and sanitize the place."

"That would be helpful."

"If it was just dirt, you could paint over it. But you can't paint over that film of smoke."

They went into the kitchen, which Sara had cleaned the previous day. You would never have known it. "I'm sorry about the mess—"

"Don't worry. I've seen worse."

"Should we replace the stove and refrigerator?"

"Not if they work."

"They work, but they're not going to last much longer."

"Then let the new owners replace them."

"What about the cabinets?"

"I wouldn't touch them. You wouldn't get your money back."

She led Peggy into the powder room, where she pointed out the broken tank cover.

"You won't be able to match the color. Pink went out of style thirty years ago. But you won't be able to guess what color the new owners will like, so don't replace the toilets and sinks."

They went upstairs and looked at the bedrooms and the full bath. The rooms needed painting, but not as badly as the downstairs rooms. And at least the toilet and the sink were blue, which wasn't such an unfashionable color.

As they headed back to the kitchen they encountered Ringer standing in the doorway looking as if he resented their intrusion.

Peggy reached down and petted him. "Does he smoke too?"

"He smells like he does. And he must enjoy cigars, or else he wouldn't stay inside."

"He must get a second-hand nicotine high."

In the kitchen Peggy said she would have no trouble selling the house as it was, provided that the rooms were cleaned and painted.

Sara lingered in the house for a while after the agent had left. The voices that had kept her awake during the night began to alternate in her head despite her efforts to tune them out. She paced from the living room to the dining room to the kitchen, considering her options. She could go and meet Brother Jeremiah and carry out the plot. She could tell him no, she wouldn't do it. Or she could just not show up.

On her way from the living room to the kitchen she stopped in the hallway and looked at the picture of Jesus that her mother had gotten her father to hang in a spot where you would see it upon entering or leaving the house, going upstairs or coming downstairs, or heading into the kitchen. Unless you avoided the hallway, you couldn't miss it.

As she gazed into the eyes of Jesus she heard the voices.

"I come not to bring peace, but to bring a sword."

"He came to bring love, not violence."

Finally she heard her own voice, which told her what to do.

When she got to the clinic she could tell from the expression on Brother Jeremiah's face that he had begun to wonder if she was coming.

"Welcome, sister. Have you come to do God's work?"

"I have. So let's get on with it."

They got coffee at the deli and then sat down on the bank that overlooked the swimming pool. The children were having the best time.

"Just set your handbag on the ground between us."

"Okay," she said obediently.

He was putting the bomb into her handbag when she became aware of people approaching from behind them.

"Hold it right there," a male voice with authority said.

She turned, and she saw several police, including the detective she had talked with, standing with their weapons drawn.

"You Judas!" Brother Jeremiah snarled at her.

"If you make even the slightest move," the detective told him, "I'll blow your head off."

With his hands raised, Brother Jeremiah launched into a tirade against Sara. "God will punish you. He'll put your family to the sword. He'll make your aunts and uncles and cousins die of famine and pestilence. He'll make your womb barren."

"It already is," she didn't say.

"Don't touch it," the detective said to a uniformed policeman who had approached Sara's handbag. "We have to wait for the bomb squad."

Two policemen helped Brother Jeremiah to his feet and immediately cuffed him.

A young policeman helped Sara, asking: "Are you all right?"

"I'm fine," she said, relieved.

"You'll have to come with us to the station," the detective said gently.

"Okay. Should I follow you in my car?"

"You better come with us."

She understood.

"Hyenas will eat the rotting corpses of your family," Brother Jeremiah ranted at her. "Their stinking remains will be dung upon the earth."

"I'm sorry," Sara told him as they were about to take him away. "I believe that Jesus came to bring love, not death and destruction."

"God wanted us to destroy that clinic."

"What if the bomb had killed a cleaning woman?"

"It wouldn't have. But even if it had, the sacrifice would have been worth it."

Sara shook her head. "The poor woman wouldn't have known what hit her. She wouldn't have had any more choice than those babies have."

"Hyenas will eat the rotting corpses of your family," Brother Jeremiah resumed.

"You have the right to remain silent," the detective told him.

"I wish you'd told me what you were doing," Marcelo said as he drove her from the Dobbs Ferry police station to where she had left her car.

"I wanted to tell you, but I had to make my own decision."

"I understand. If you'd done what someone advised you to do, you'd always wonder what you would have done on your own. But still—"

"I know. And I promise never to do that again."

"Well, you don't have to promise."

"I want to promise. And now I *can* promise because I won't need to do that again."

"I understand," he said, slowing the car.

They went to bed early. She snuggled up against Marcelo and soon fell asleep. In a dream she heard Brother Jeremiah's voice telling her she was a Judas, she heard her mother's voice telling her she was a good girl, and she heard God's voice telling her she would have a baby. In this dream God wasn't talking to her husband, He was talking to her. And when she awoke she still laughed, but it was a different kind of laughter.

The following day she stopped to talk with Father Paul in front of the church.

"Did you hear what happened at the clinic?" he asked.

It had been on the local television news, which reported that the plot had been foiled by an unnamed woman.

"I was involved in it. Would you like to know the details?"

"Are you wanting to make a confession?"

"No. I'm wanting," she said, imitating his Irish brogue, "to tell you about it."

"Then tell me about it," he said, smiling appreciatively.

She told him how Brother Jeremiah had enlisted her. "He was very persuasive. He made me feel like I'd been chosen to do God's work."

"How did he justify committing an act of violence?"

"He quoted Jesus where He said 'I come not to bring peace, but to bring a sword.' He claimed that Jesus meant that literally."

"Some people believe He did mean it literally."

"What do you believe?"

"I believe He meant it metaphorically."

"That's what I decided. But for a while I did have doubts."

"How did you reach your decision?"

"By looking into the eyes of Jesus. When you look into the eyes of people," Sara explained, "you can tell what they mean."

"For what it's worth," Father Paul said, "I think you made the right interpretation. But let me give you another angle—"

She waited to hear it.

"Are you familiar with the Book of Kells?"

"I'm not familiar with it, but I've heard of it. It's an Irish copy of the Gospels, right?"

"Right. It's written in Latin, as everything was in those days. The Latin word for sword is *gladius*. That's where the word gladiator comes from. So in Latin the statement your monk quoted would be '*Non veni pacem mittere sed gladium*.' But instead of the word *gladium* the Book of Kells uses the word *gaudium*, which means joy."

Sara smiled. "So Jesus really said 'I come not to bring peace, but to bring joy?' "

"According to the Book of Kells He did. But I prefer to translate it as 'I come not only to bring peace but also joy.' "

"I prefer that too."

After taking a drag on his cigarette Father Paul asked: "Where did you look into the eyes of Jesus? In a dream?"

"No. In my father's house. There's a picture of Jesus hanging on the wall."

"Then you've been rewarded for taking care of your father."

"I guess I have. But speaking of dreams, you remember the one in which God told my husband I'd have a baby?"

"Yes, I remember."

"Well, I had another dream like it, only this time God was talking to me."

"That sounds like progress," Father Paul said, smiling. "What did He tell you?"

"He told me I would have a baby."

"And what are the odds of that happening?"

"Almost zero. So it would be a miracle."

"Are you hoping for a miracle?"

"I'm always hoping. But I told you," Sara said, "we decided to adopt. And now that I've dealt with Brother Jeremiah, I'm ready to go ahead with it."

"God bless you."

"Thank you, father."

On the first Saturday of August she had lunch with Regina, whom she hadn't seen in more than two months. Regina had been occupied in buying a house and moving into it. The house was on Park Avenue, north of Shonnard Place, and less than a mile from Sara's house.

They couldn't think of a restaurant that was equally distant from their houses, so they agreed to meet at O'Malley's on Lake Avenue, which was in Regina's neighborhood.

It was a typical Irish pub, and when Sara walked in she felt as if she were back in Woodlawn, except that her father wasn't there. Regina was already there and had taken a booth, so Sara headed directly toward her.

She noticed that Regina didn't have a cigarette, and as she sat down she asked: "Have you given up smoking?"

Regina nodded. "For the duration."

"The duration of what?" she almost asked, and then it hit her. "You're pregnant?"

Regina nodded again vigorously. "It finally happened. And you know what? I'm sure it happened the first night in our own house."

"So all you needed was to get away from Joe's mother?"

"She was the problem."

"I'm so happy for you," Sara said, leaning across the table and hugging her friend. For a long time they shared a delicious feeling of happiness.

"Can I get you something to drink?" the waiter asked.

Regina ordered a soda, and Sara ordered a glass of white wine.

"Now, what's happening with your father?"

Sara brought her friend up to date. "I'm trying to sell his house now. We moved his furniture over to Woodlawn, but there're still a lot of things in the house that we have to get rid of before we can have it cleaned and painted."

"It sounds like you're expecting someone to help you."

"Marcelo will help me. He always helps me. But I'm hoping my sister will help me too. A lot of the things belong to her."

"Has she ever helped you do anything?"

"No. Well, let me take that back," Sara said upon reflecting. "My sister helped me discover something about myself."

"You mean by getting pregnant?"

"Remember how we talked about the idea of her giving me the baby? Well, she offered it to me, and we made a deal. I thought it was the answer to my prayers."

"So what happened?"

Sara would have liked to tell her friend the whole truth, but she decided against it since there were things you had to keep in the family. "She lost the baby."

"I'm sorry," Regina said, reaching out to her.

"You were right when you told me not to get my hopes up."

Regina held her hand in consolation for a while, and then she asked: "What did you discover?"

"I discovered what I'm capable of doing when I'm angry."

"You were angry over losing the baby?"

"Yes. And now that I know what I'm capable of doing, I have a better understanding of my sister."

"I hope you didn't do anything out of anger."

"I didn't. But it was only by the grace of God that I didn't," Sara added humbly.

At that moment the waiter came to take their orders. They both ordered hamburgers and French fries.

"Since your father moved back to Woodlawn," Regina said, "and you're not under pressure from him every day, you might get pregnant."

"I might, but I'm not going to count on it. We're going ahead with our plan to adopt a baby."

"Will you look in Latin America?"

"Yeah. I have a former roommate who lives in Colombia, and Marcelo knows some people in Brazil."

"What about the Dominican Republic?"

"Of course we'll look there. But it's not easy to adopt a baby from there."

"Why not? They have a lot of babies, don't they?"

"There's no shortage. But they don't like to give them up."

After lunch she followed Regina to Park Avenue. The house was red brick, with minimal wood, so it was maintenance free. Regina gave her a tour, and Sara could tell that Joe's mother hadn't played a role in decorating it. The style of the furniture was traditional, like a display room at Ethan Allen.

"This house is perfect for you," Sara said when they had completed the tour.

"I like it, and Joe likes it."

"What about his mother? Does she like it?"

"She thinks it doesn't have enough bedrooms."

"It has three bedrooms, which is enough for three or four children. How many children does she expect you to have?"

"In this house she expects us to have only one child, or two of a kind. She wants us to have a bedroom for her."

Sara laughed. "Well, that'll give you an incentive to have at least three children."

"A major incentive," Regina agreed.

Moving the furniture was the easy part, though her father resisted her policy to dispose of pieces that he wouldn't need. They dickered to the last end table, with Sara yielding when it became emotional and her father yielding when it became clear that the piece wouldn't fit into his new apartment.

Now that the house was clear of furniture she could see what unpleasant tasks remained—it was as if the tide had gone out, revealing what lay on the bottom of the ocean. She started with the kitchen. She had already packed and moved the equipment for cooking and eating, but she hadn't yet touched the supplies that her father had accumulated in the cabinets over the years. There were enough boxes of plastic wrap and aluminum foil to last through a nuclear winter. There were plastic containers and aluminum containers of all shapes and sizes.

She spent two days in the kitchen emptying the cabinets and putting the items into wine cartons that the owner of the liquor store on Palisade had kindly given her. She ended up with twenty boxes, which a big guy she had found through Peggy hauled away in his pickup truck. And then she emptied the basement, which took her another two days.

The last and the most dreaded task was cleaning out the attic. Before undertaking it, Sara asked Becky to help her, and she was surprised when her sister responded positively and even took a day off from work.

To reach the attic you had to pull a chain that dangled from a trap door, which then unfolded into a ladder. Sara went up and confronted the hot, dusty air.

"You don't have to come up here," she told her sister. "I'll hand things down to you."

"What's up there?"

"A lot of boxes. It looks like mom saved everything."

"I wonder if she saved my papers."

"I'm sure she did," Sara said. Her sister had won awards for her papers, and their mother was justly proud of them.

It took them the morning to bring all the boxes down from the attic. At that point they took a break and walked over to Palisade to get coffee from the deli.

Upon returning to the house they sat on the floor of the bedroom where they had gathered the boxes from the attic and drank the coffee. They talked about their father's move back to Woodlawn, avoiding sore subjects until Becky asked: "Did you hear what happened at the abortion clinic in Dobbs Ferry?"

"I heard some guy tried to blow it up."

"They said he was a monk."

"He was dressed like a monk. I used to see him with the protesters when I drove by."

"I can understand why he wanted to destroy it. And I wish he had. I wish someone had destroyed the clinic that did my abortion before I went there."

"Would that have stopped you?"

"I don't know. I hope it would have."

They went back to work, sitting on the carpet, each of them dealing with a box of things their mother had saved.

They had gone through about half of the boxes when Becky stopped.

"What's wrong?" Sara asked. There were tears streaming from her sister's eyes.

"I found your dolls. And I see what I did to them."

Sara felt a pain that was like what she imagined her father felt from the piece of shrapnel in his leg, except that it was in her heart. She watched as her sister lifted what had been her favorite doll out of the box. She had taken such good care of this doll. And then one day she had found it on the floor with its face smashed, its hair pulled out, its clothes torn, and its limbs broken as if it had been a hapless victim of marauding barbarians.

"How could I have done this?" Becky sobbed.

"You were acting out of anger," Sara told her. "And I can understand it. I couldn't before, but I can now."

"Will you ever forgive me?"

"I already have."

On hands and knees Sara went to her sister. They hugged each other, and for the first time Sara felt love flowing toward her sister. She felt love flowing both ways.

Two weeks before school started she and Marcelo went to the Dominican Republic, where he had aunts and uncles and cousins and nieces and nephews. Wanting privacy and not wanting to impose on his family, they rented an apartment in Santa Cruz, a small town twenty minutes west of Puerto Plata, where they had stayed on previous visits.

Santa Cruz had a beach that was sheltered by an outlying reef, so the waves were gentle and the water was safe for swimming. Marcelo's relatives joined them on the beach, and they would sit around in rented chairs, eating the food and drinking the beverages that they had brought with them, and keeping an eye on the children.

There were so many babies. Wherever Sara looked she saw a baby, and she was often handed a baby to hold for a while. But sooner or later she had to give the baby back since it belonged to someone. Every baby belonged to someone, and even if it didn't have a mother, there was someone available in the extended family to adopt it and raise it. So Sara didn't get her hopes up about finding a baby here.

One afternoon, as they were relaxing on the beach with Marcelo's relatives from Santiago, she was handed a baby to hold for a while. It was a baby girl, who couldn't have been more than three months old, and Sara's heart went out to her.

"She's adorable," Sara said. "Who does she belong to?"

"She doesn't belong to anyone," Marcelo said. "Her parents were killed in an accident."

"The poor thing." She gazed into the baby's big brown eyes. "What's her name?"

"María Altagracia."

"What a lovely name. It suits her perfectly."

A cousin, whose name was Yudelka, said: "It's a miracle that she's alive. She was riding on a *motoconcho* with her parents. Her mother was sitting behind her father, holding her. And the driver hit a hole in the road. They all went flying, and the baby flew out of her mother's arms. Her parents smashed into a truck, but the baby flew to the side of the road, where a young man caught her. She wasn't even scratched."

"I told you," Sara could hear her father saying, "Dominicans have fast hands, so they play well in the infield."

"God had a purpose for saving her," Yudelka said.

"She means," Marcelo said, "that if we want her, the baby's ours. They brought her for us."

"Why would they give her to us?"

"You and I are family."

"María Altagracia," she said to the baby. "You're our gift from God. Do you know that, sweetie?"

The baby smiled with joy in her eyes.

"In my dream God said I'd have a baby. So this is what He meant. It's the miracle we were praying for."

"Yes. It is," Marcelo said, laying his hand on the baby's shoulder and tenderly kissing the back of her neck.

Sara waited for her mother's voice, ready for a comment or a question. Instead, she received a silent blessing.

BOOK CLUB GUIDE TO

Sara's Laughter

Tom Milton

An introduction to *Sara's Laughter*

Sara is the older of two sisters who were raised in Woodlawn, an Irish neighborhood in the Bronx. Sara is happy and social, whereas her sister Becky is unhappy and antisocial. Driven by envy, Becky has repeatedly done malicious things to Sara like disfiguring her dolls and trashing her high school yearbook and sabotaging her relationships with men. At the same time Becky has always tried to outshine Sara by getting better grades and making more money.

Their father, who fought with the marines at Guadalcanal, was a lineman with the phone company, and their mother was a traditional housewife. They lived in the two-family house in which their father was born, initially with his parents on the ground floor and later with tenants. The girls went to parochial schools and to Fordham University, where their mother hoped they would find husbands, and then they got jobs in Manhattan, where for a while they shared an apartment.

Though her mother keeps warning Sara that if she waits too long to select a husband the good men will all be taken, Sara is determined to wait until she finds the right man for her. When she finally does find him there are two complications: the man is married, and he isn't white. The first complication is more easily resolved since Marcelo is in the process of getting an annulment of a marriage that was never consummated. And except for not being white Marcelo has all the qualities her parents could have wanted in a husband for their daughter, including the fact that he really loves her, not to mention the fact that he is a physician, so the second complication doesn't stop Sara's parents from accepting Marcelo as a son-in-law, though it lingers in her father's fear of having a black grandson.

With her older daughter married and her younger daughter doing well at a job on Wall Street, their mother gets their father to sell the two-family house in Woodlawn and buy a single-family house in the neighborhood of Yonkers where she grew up and where most of her old friends still live. But within a year their mother dies of a heart attack, and their father is stranded in a neighborhood where he has no friends.

Concerned about him, Sara and Marcelo sell their condo in Manhattan and buy a house in Yonkers that is close enough to her father so that they can take care of him but far enough away so that at least they have some privacy. By now Sara has dropped out of corporate life, where she worked as a buyer for a national retailer, and she is a third-grade teacher at a parochial school within walking distance of her house. Marcelo is working at a clinic in the neighborhood of the Bronx where he grew up, so their house is in a good location for both of them.

Meanwhile, Becky has married a man she met in a bar and is living in Tribeca in an apartment she bought for "only" three and a half million dollars. She flies back and forth from New York to London, promoting the trade of complex securities that she has designed, while her husband Bart owns a wine store in Tribeca that she bought for him.

By now their father has retired from the phone company, and he is commuting daily to Woodlawn, where he hangs out at a neighborhood bar with his old friends. He cannot understand why neither of his daughters has given him a grandson, and he refuses to believe there is any physical reason why Sara can't have a baby, though she has patiently explained the reason to him—an advanced case of endometriosis.

Sara is being treated by a famous doctor in Manhattan who specializes in fertility problems, and she is willing to try anything, including methods that aren't approved by her church. Though her doctor has told her the odds of an embryo surviving in her are almost zero, she keeps trying and hoping for a miracle. Her hope is kept alive by a dream in which God told her husband she would have a baby. When Becky, who doesn't want to have children, gets pregnant accidentally from an extramarital fling, Sara comes up with a solution that would finally make her dream come true. But when things don't go according to plan she loses her way, and she discovers a side of her nature she never imagined.

A conversation with Tom Milton

I was comfortably settling into a good read about a woman's relationships with her husband, her mother, her father, her sister, and a friend, and about her efforts to have a baby, but having read your previous novels, I expected her to have a public mission.

Sara has a personal mission, but it evolves as things happen.

Her personal mission is to have a baby, and you put an obstacle in her way—an advanced case of endometriosis.

A lot of women Sara's age have such obstacles, which they didn't expect to have.

Sara's mother tells her she wouldn't have had a problem if she hadn't waited so long to get married.

And Sara argues with her mother, insisting that the only reason she waited was to find the right man.

But there were a few complications when she found him, including the fact that he wasn't white. You dealt with the issue of racism in some of your other novels, but here you put it in another context.

In this context it's not about civil rights, it's about the extent to which parents accept interracial marriage for their children.

Sara's mother seems very accepting. Of course it helps that Marcelo is a doctor, and that her mother is beginning to wonder if Sara will ever get married. Her father has a bigger problem.

I think no matter which men their daughters marry, fathers have a bigger problem.

The relationship between Sara and her father is a variation of the daughter-father relationship that was central in three of your other novels: The Admiral's Daughter, All the Flowers, *and* A Shower of Roses. *You're obviously fascinated with that relationship.*

So were the ancient Greek dramatists. It has a lot of potential for drama.

I noticed that the daughters have one thing in common—they're all the oldest children in their families.

They are. And in that position they challenge their fathers, they question the values of their fathers.

In your novels the conflicts between the daughters and their fathers have societal dimensions.

The conflicts are over social issues that I want to examine and make people more aware of.

Sara is under pressure from her father to give him a grandson, and in using medical technology to help her conceive, she runs into the limits set by the doctrine of her church. I know you have a reason for subjecting Sara to this conflict.

It raises a lot of issues. Do people have a right to have their own children? Should they pursue having their own children no matter what it takes? Should people do anything that technology makes possible?

There are issues in using technology for this purpose, but there are also issues in adopting a child, as Sara's friend Regina points out.

Yes, either way there are issues. Regina's issue is not knowing what you get when you adopt a child.

Let's talk more about Sara's father. Like so many men, he depends on women to take care of him, and when his wife suddenly dies he shifts the responsibility to his daughter.

He expects women to take care of him. But he's not a mama's boy, he's a ladies' man. And he's a member of the "greatest generation." He went to war, he came back and got a job and raised a family and never complained about the big things, only about the little things.

There are times when you catch glimpses of how much he appreciates Sara, but he really doesn't show it much.

As Sara's mother says, he has a good heart, but he's tough on people, and he holds them to high standards.

The other relationship that fascinated me was the one between Sara and her sister Becky.

It's the old story about how one child envies another for a relationship with a parent.

Sara is clearly her father's favorite, and Becky feels close to their mother. But Sara is the one who hears her mother's voice in her head.

Sara has a major issue with her mother that wasn't resolved before her mother died.

And her sister has an unresolved issue with Sara.

That's what makes families so interesting, their unresolved issues.

The plot is driven by these unresolved issues, so your novel is about much more than a woman trying to have a baby.

It's about how people deal with their unresolved issues.

Before I let you go, I have a question. Can you tell me why Sara laughed when God told her she would have a baby?

When her students read the story of Abraham and Sarah in class, one of them asks her the same question.

And she does what a good teacher does—she asks her students why they think Sarah laughed.

So why do you think my Sara laughed?

I don't know. I think she laughed because she felt blessed.

Well, let's see why the other readers think she laughed.

Discussion questions

1. To what extent is Sara influenced by the voice of her mother in her head?

2. What's the difference between the messages Sara gets from her mother and her father about her inability to get pregnant?

3. What issues does Sara confront as she uses the technology available to women who have fertility problems?

4. Evaluate the advice that Sara gets from Dr. Vesely.

5. How would you describe Sara's relationship with her mother?

6. Does Sara achieve separation from her mother?

7. Sara's sister accuses her of being daddy's little girl. Is this a valid accusation?

8. Why is Marcelo the right man for Sara?

9. Marcelo has two complications: he is married, and he isn't white. Which complication is harder for Sara's mother to deal with? What does that tell us about her mother?

10. How deep do you think her father's racism is?

11. Would Becky have been a different person if she had been an only child?

12. Explain Becky's behavior after she got pregnant.

13. What do you think of Sara's solution to her sister's problem?

14. What perspectives do we gain from Sara's conversations at lunch with her friend Regina?

15. What perspectives do we gain from Sara's conversations with Father Paul?

16. How does Sara's view of the local abortion clinic evolve during the story?

17. Would Sara have joined the protesters in front of the clinic solely as a matter of principle?

18. Why is Sara mesmerized by Brother Jeremiah?

19. What did Sara and Becky discover about themselves that changed their relationship?

20. Do any miracles occur in this story?

21. Why did Sara laugh when God told her she would have a baby?